FRAT BOY CONFESSIONS

NATHAN BAY

First edition: October 2022
Bay Cove Press
ISBN: 9798357061874

CONTENTS

INTRODUCTION

A NOTE FROM THE PRESIDENT OF BETA GAMMA ZETA

Can you keep a secret?

You're about to meet the guys of Beta Gamma Zeta here in sunny California. They're my bros, my amigos, my partners in crime. And they have some exciting stories to share with you.

Our fraternity is a place for fun. Sometimes we give each other a hard time, but deep down, we love each other. The house gives us the freedom to bond and share a special sort of intimacy. There's no fear of labels or judgment here. It's all about what makes people feel good. After you've read these stories, I hope you feel good, too.

So settle in, get comfortable, and join the bros for some pillow talk. A happy ending is guaranteed.

Chad Johnson
President of Beta Gamma Zeta

PITCHING A TENT

CHAPTER 1

"Alright, are you ready to do this?" My roommate and future fraternity brother, Jarrod, hoists his sleeping bag onto his back. Another bag, which holds a pop-up tent folded down to miraculously small proportions, is slung over his shoulder.

"Yeah, ready as I'll ever be," I answer, carrying my own sleeping bag on my shoulder, a mini cooler in one hand, and a bag full of snacks and essentials hanging from the other hand.

But actually no, I'm not ready at all. This is a horrible idea. I can't believe I am going through with this camping trip.

There are only two very simple rules to follow:

1. Survive a night in the "haunted" forest.

2. Take selfies outside our tent every hour on the hour until dawn.

If we complete this mission, we'll be initiated into the fraternity of Beta Gamma Zeta. If we fail, we'll be stuck with toilet cleaning duties for an entire month, after which we'll receive one final opportunity to pledge again. *Parole*, they call it.

I'm not an outdoorsy person, nor am I a fan of haunted houses, or haunted forests, for that matter. But I really want to join this fraternity. And it's just one night, I tell myself. Camping in the woods couldn't be nearly as bad as some of the hazing horror stories I'd heard from other fraternities.

Chad Johnson, the chapter president of Beta Gamma Zeta, checks the seats of his jeep to make sure we haven't left anything behind. "Last chance to back out, ladies," he says with a snort.

"We'll be fine," Jarrod says.

Chad stares him down for a second, then smiles wickedly. "Good. Call if you need anything."

I check my phone. The words *No Service* are displayed in the top corner. "Is there cell reception in these woods?"

Chad shakes his head. "Nope."

"Then how can we—?"

"I said we'll be fine," Jarrod growls.

"I'll be back here at 6 AM to pick you guys up." Chad gets in his jeep and slams the door. Without another word, he peels out from the gravel turnabout and takes off toward the highway.

"That guy thinks he's such hot shit," Jarrod mutters. "Come on, Ian, let's go. It's a mile hike to the campsite."

I follow behind my hulking frat brother without arguing. He's clearly the confrontational type. I'm not sure he's doing us any favors by getting into a pissing contest with Chad. But at least I feel better knowing we'll be camping together. I'd never survive these woods on my own. Of that much, I am certain.

The terrain is kind of steep. We seem to be walking sideways down the grassy hilltop, one bumpy step at a time. I never feel like I can really get my footing, and my arm is already getting sore from the heavy bag I'm carrying.

The hike seems to have no effect on Jarrod, who is built like a stack of bricks on legs. I'm in pretty good shape, slim with an athletic build, but admittedly it's been a while since I've worked out, and I am definitely feeling it.

"So you really think this place is haunted?" I call ahead to Jarrod, who is soon outpacing me, the distance between us growing wider.

He looks over his shoulder and slows down just a hair. "Probably."

"Wait, what?"

"Just kidding." Jarrod chuckles but keeps moving.

"I read that people have died out here."

"People have died everywhere. You think we're the first humans to walk on this land?"

I furrow my brow, surprised at how succinctly my roomie can make a point. "I...hadn't thought of it that way."

He shrugs. "Thousands of people have lived and died everywhere you step. Ghosts are all around, if you believe in that sort of stuff. There's nothing special about these woods."

I don't think Jarrod would be up for a debate, so I decide to let the subject go. Still, the woods do have a history. Strange sightings, freak accidents, a couple of unexplained fires. He'd probably say there is a logical explanation for all of those events.

As if sensing my apprehension, Jarrod stops and turns to face me. His bushy eyebrows draw together at the bridge of his chiseled nose. "Ian, we're in this together, bud. Are you going to be able to hold up your end of the deal?"

"Yep, absolutely."

He doesn't seem convinced, and neither am I.

It's just one night...

I take stock of our surroundings, figuring I might as well enjoy our trek through nature since I don't plan on camping ever again. The leaves are changing to red and orange, and the hills are bathed in golden light from the setting sun. I take a deep breath, noting the crisp September air. Maybe this won't be so bad.

"So, what's your story, newbie?" Jarrod asks as he forges ahead.

"I'm no more a newbie than you are," I say with a laugh.

"My brother was in Beta Gamma Zeta. My real brother," Jarrod clarifies. "I've been partying with the fraternity since I was a sophomore in high school."

"Oh, got it." He's put me in my place once again. "Is there anything I should know about the guys?"

"They're mostly good people. Loyal to the end, that's what my brother says. Chad's a real dick, though. Watch your back around him. Actually, watch your front too. He loves to swat guys in the nuts."

"Why?"

"Because it's fun." Jarrod turns and makes a quick leap toward my crotch with his open palm. I jump out of the way, just missing as he grazes the inside of my thigh. He smiles and bursts out laughing. "Good reflexes, newbie."

"I'm beginning to wonder if Chad's the real troublemaker. Maybe it's you."

"Never know." Jarrod winks at me, his pink tongue darting out between his teeth. "So, I asked what your story was."

"There's not much to say." *It's too soon to tell him my secret.* "I moved here from a little town a couple of hours away. Got accepted into two colleges, but my other choice was too far away and too expensive."

"You don't really seem like the type to join a fraternity."

"Like you said, Beta Gamma Zetas are loyal to the end. I like the idea of joining a brotherhood for life. I'm an only child, so it'd be nice to have some ties outside my parents."

"Makes sense." Jarrod squints off into the distance. "I think we're just down the hill here."

I pull out a crudely drawn map. "Yeah, looks like there's a small creek that feeds into a river. I can see the water."

"Did you think I was lying?"

"No, I—" There is no winning with this guy. He always has to have the upper hand. "I didn't mean anything by it. I was just agreeing that we were getting closer to the spot."

Jarrod continues ahead of me. Each step he takes exudes confident, frat bro energy. He will be right at home with the rest of our house. But despite his cocky attitude, I can't deny his appeal. He has blazing blue eyes that pierce my soul. If he ever doubted himself or second-guessed his choices, I'd never know it. He is always in control, always taking command. A natural-born leader.

And he is hot as hell.

I've been insanely attracted to Jarrod from the moment we met. Sharing a room with him only intensified my feelings. Thankfully I've been too busy to think about him most of the time.

Settling in as a college freshman is a new experience for me. I've never lived away from home, never had to share anything, what with being an only child. And my schedule seems to have been organized by a masochist. Every class takes place on an opposite end of campus. I am racing back and forth here and there, down sidewalks, up stairs, through hallways, with only ten minutes between classes. With all the changes in my life over the past month, I'm usually too tired to think about the temptation sleeping in the bed only a few feet away from where I lay. But now we're all alone, and I'll have nothing but my thoughts to consume me.

We follow a path down the hill and under a dense canopy of trees. Suddenly everything feels different in the atmosphere. The world grows a little darker, the air a bit cooler. And the woods are eerily quiet. Shouldn't birds be chirping? Squirrels chittering? All I can hear is the crackle of our footsteps among the dead leaves.

"Over there, by the scorched tree." Jarrod nods toward our destination.

A feeling of dread twists my stomach into knots. We set our bags next to the battered trunk, which looks like it could disintegrate at any moment. Most of the tree's foliage had been burnt to ashes. What is left of its limbs protrudes like charred bones.

"You know, a man died right here last year," I point out. "He was burned to death."

"Did you think I didn't know that?"

I fight back an exasperated sigh. "We don't have to sleep in this exact spot. It's not like the guys will know if the tent isn't right here." I tilt my head toward some normal looking trees that don't scream death. "How about over there?"

"Fine, I guess you're right." Jarrod picks up our bags and moves them under the cluster of trees. "The guys just said we had to sleep *by* the scorched tree, not directly next to it."

Wait a minute. Did Mr. Know-It-All actually admit I was right? Score one point for Ian.

I pull out two bottles of water, offering one to Jarrod. "Care for a drink?" He gratefully accepts, then raises the lip of his black tank top and wipes his face. His abdominal muscles, gleaming with the sheen of sweat, clench and flex. I feel myself grow rock-hard in an instant, hypnotized by the view of Jarrod's exposed torso.

"Ian, did you hear me?" he asks.

"Sorry, what?" I try to blink away the cloud of desire swirling in my head. "I must have zoned out."

"No worries. I was saying we should go for a swim."

I tear my eyes away from the dark trail of curls that dances down to the waistband of Jarrod's shorts. "Swimming?"

"Yeah, you know. That thing you do in water. Paddling, kicking one foot behind the other." He makes a show of moving his arms and legs to demonstrate. "They call that swimming."

My cheeks feel flushed. "Right, of course." I try to conceal my protruding wood by holding the bottle of water in front of me. If Jarrod notices, my secret will come out. "I didn't bring any swim trunks."

"Swim trunks. Bro, seriously?" Jarrod laughs and takes a swig of water. I watch his glistening lips tighten around the bottle top. "You don't need swim trunks. We're out in the wild."

Wild. That's what I feel when I imagine skinny dipping in the creek with Jarrod. Suddenly spending the night in the haunted woods doesn't seem so scary. There are darker disasters that loom on the horizon.

I fear I'll never make it to dawn.

CHAPTER 2

Jarrod is already peeling off his shirt before we get down to the water. He hops on one leg as he pulls off a shoe, then the other shoe, and then slides down his socks. He makes quick work with the rest of his clothes, and in the blink of an eye, everything he wore is carelessly abandoned in the grass. All I can comprehend is a whirlwind of perfectly sculpted muscles dressed in dense body hair. Just before he's out of sight, I catch a fleeting glimpse of his thick butt cheeks.

He splashes into the water with a relieved howl. "Ahhh, that feels so much better."

I stand awkwardly on the creekside, willing myself to go soft, and kind of wishing he'd somehow forget I'm there. But no such luck. His penetrating eyes fixate on me. "What are you waiting for? Come in and join me. The water feels great."

"Yeah, okay." I raise my shirt over my head. My nipples grow stiff when a breeze kisses my bare chest. My roommate's eyes remained focused on me, and insecurity consumes me. "Dude, stop being gay," I snap. "You don't have to watch."

"Damn, sorry Ian. I didn't mean to make you uncomfortable." He turns away quickly.

I feel guilty for my angst-ridden outburst, but at least I've bought myself some privacy. I quickly undress, look down and see that I'm still half-hard. Thankfully Jarrod keeps his face turned, looking off into the distance. I leap toward the creek and swim out until the water rises past my waist.

"Sorry," I say, wading over to Jarrod's side. "I didn't mean to be rude. I was just...you know, self-conscious. You look like you—" I gesture across the expanse of his body. "And I look like, well, me."

He smiles assuringly, though I'm not sure I deserve his kindness. "No need to be self-conscious, man. You have a great body." He studies me in a way that makes my heart tremble. "You're so smooth too. Do you shave?"

"No." I cross my arms across my chest. "I've just never been very hairy." Most of my body is naturally smooth, and the fine blond blades on my arms can barely be seen. "I kind of wish I had more hair like you."

"Are you kidding? I feel like a grizzly bear." Jarrod points to the dark swirls that circle his pink nipples. "I've tried trimming it all off but then I just feel prickly. And it itches like hell too."

I nod. "Yeah, I guess that would suck. But still—"

"Like I said, you're a real catch," Jarrod adds with finality. "Be proud of how you look."

His flattery is turning my knees to jelly. It was one thing to think of him as a bossy jock who always had to have the last word. I put up with guys like him all through high school. But now he's being nice to me, checking out my body, telling me things he likes about it. This is doing nothing to tame the wild desire that burns deep inside me, not to mention that we are alone and naked side-by-side.

Without warning, he dunks his head underwater, and my breath hitches in my throat, afraid of what he'll see down below. But he returns to the surface just as fast, smoothing back his lush black hair and scrubbing the sweat from his face.

"Better?" I ask.

"Much." He flashes his dazzling smile my way and chuckles. "You should try it."

I take his advice and dive underwater. That's when I catch an up-close view of what hangs between his legs. Damn, it's even bigger than I imagined. Long and thick. I shudder as I wonder how much I could fit between my lips.

When I rise back to the surface, I know I have to think of something to distract me. "So, Jarrod, uh, what do you like to do?"

"For fun?"

"Yeah." I try to look casual while I secretly tame a stomach full of butterflies. "It seems like we only see each other coming and going back at the house. We haven't really had a chance to talk."

His eyes sweep across me as if he's sizing me up. What did I say wrong? Was it the way I said it?

"I like soccer," he says finally. "And pizza. And beer. I like working out. I have to do it more often these days, you know, on account of the pizza and beer." He pats his insanely ripped stomach and laughs. "I guess that's it. How 'bout you?"

"I like reading. Haven't had much time to read since school started." Panic suddenly strikes as I worry he'll ask what kind of books I read. My Kindle is full of porny titles, which will surely give me away. I quickly switch to a less loaded subject. "Oh, um, I like animals. That's actually what I hope to pursue, a degree in veterinary medicine."

"That's pretty cool. Do you have any pets at home?"

"Nah." I rub the back of my neck, thankful he didn't probe my reading habits. "I'm allergic to pet dander."

Jarrod raises his eyebrows, giving me that same frustratingly judgmental expression everyone gives when they find out about my allergy. When will I learn to just lie?

His perfect lips spread into that annoyingly smug grin he always wears. "Uh, Ian, buddy, you understand what veterinarians do, right?"

"Yes, of course. What can I say? It's a curse. I love animals but my nose didn't get the memo. My allergy is mild, really. Antihistamines help. And a vet's office isn't nearly as bad for allergies as you'd think. The exam tables are cleaned between every appointment, the floors are swept several times a day and mopped every night by the cleaning crew. It's nothing at all like having pets in your home, where their dander gets into your rugs, your sofas, and all that. I did an internship this past summer at a vet's office and it was awesome. What about you? What are you studying?"

He shrugs a meaty shoulder. "Haven't decided yet. Something in business or finance. My dad owns a couple of tech companies. I always thought it would be cool to do the same, but I haven't quite figured out my passion yet."

That was unexpected. The brawny jock actually has goals. "Yeah, you've got time to figure it out," I say.

"So, do you have a girlfriend?"

"Definitely not," I answer too quickly.

"Why do you say it like that?"

"Oh, I mean... No reason."

"Hey, I'm an open-minded guy. You can tell me if you're gay."

"Good to know." I scan our surroundings, desperate to find a way out of this conversation. "Hey, looks like we're losing daylight. Maybe we should get the tent set up before it's dark."

Jarrod nods, but doesn't appear satisfied with my abrupt change of subject. Thankfully he starts swimming toward land without pressing me further. It takes every ounce of my willpower not to stare as he ascends from the water.

Maybe once we get back to our campsite, I can sneak off and give myself a quick one-handed salute. That should take some of the edge off all this tension I feel for my hot roommate.

CHAPTER 3

Life back at camp isn't doing anything to calm my nerves. Instead of putting his clothes back on, Jarrod is strutting around in just his boxer shorts and shoes. Meanwhile I'm walking around soaked to the bone with my wet clothes uncomfortably clinging to my every move.

We take a quick selfie with my phone, part of our hourly duty to document our time in the woods. Jarrod leans in close to me for the shot. His bare shoulder presses against mine, and I hold back a needy sigh as I force a smile for the camera.

We make fast progress with the tent. It's a basic pop-up model that supposedly takes less than 20 minutes to configure, according to the sleeve. Jarrod is deft at getting the rods connected. I offer very little help, occasionally pushing or pulling or holding something in place when he instructs me.

Our new abode is scant, but it will have to do. The roof is mostly mesh, offering plenty of airflow and ventilation. The interior is large enough to fit two adults, plus a little extra room for our bags, and not much else.

I check my phone. Still no signal, but at least I can check the time. It's half past six. The sun is glowing through the trees, casting eerie shadows all around us.

Jarrod sits down on a nearby log, legs spread casually, and I catch a glimpse of his plump balls inside the leg opening of his boxers.

"Hey, I gotta go somewhere and relieve myself," I say.

Jarrod nods to some nearby trees. "Go take a piss over there."

I grit my teeth, agitated that he thinks I need instructions on using the bathroom. "Actually, I need to do more than that. I think I'm gonna head down toward that cave I saw by the creek."

His eyes flick to me. "The cave?"

"Yeah, why?"

He shrugs and returns his attention to a game he's started playing on his phone. "You don't need my permission, bro. Knock yourself out."

"I wasn't asking permission, I was just communicating with you." I bite my lip, fighting back the urge to tell Jarrod he really needs to work on his tone. "I'll be back soon."

"Have fun." His eyes remain focused on his phone. At least that should guarantee me some privacy.

I make my way down the hill. The woods seem to swallow me up as the shadows grow taller. I'm shaking with nervous energy, but I'm sure jacking off will make me feel better.

The inside of the cave is dark and smells musty. I can hear the steady drip of water somewhere beyond the darkness. This is as far as I dare to go.

I look around, confirming I'm alone. This whole place gives me the creeps, but I'll make it quick.

My cock is already rigid when I free it from my shorts. I exhale with relief, feeling the cool air on my balls. I close my eyes and let my thoughts roam free.

All I can think about is Jarrod. I hate it that I want him so bad. I hate the way his juicy pink lips curl every time he thinks he's made a witty remark, or offered some clever commentary. I hate the way his sapphire blue eyes penetrate me, like he has x-ray vision. He can see everything I'm hiding.

I spit in my hand, get it nice and slick, then sweep my palm across my sensitive cock head. A shiver travels down my back. I start working my shaft, squeezing it and stroking up and down in rhythm.

Jock Jarrod, with his monster cock and his meaty pecs. Just a big mountain of muscle and masculinity. All that hair, all over his damn body. I bet licking him would be like licking a bear. I grunt at the thought, wondering if I'd need to pop a Claritin just to bury my face in all that fur.

I'd do it, though. I'd do it in an instant. Bury my face between those ginormous pecs, lick and bite his nipples until he was begging for mercy, then I'd tongue my way down the cliffs of his abs, all the way down that fun trail below his belly button.

"Oh, fuck, Ian," he'd gasp. "I can't take anymore. Please put me in your mouth."

But I wouldn't. Not yet.

I'd take a deep inhale of his crotch, really breathe him in until the smell of his sweaty nuts filled my sinuses. His scent would be inescapable, that heaving heap of hotness.

Then I'd finally allow him some relief as I took his raging hard dick in my mouth. I might have to unhinge my jaw just to do it, but it would be worth it. I'd swallow him down to his low hangers. Swallow him until I couldn't breathe, till I was choking on his massive cock. I'd look up at him through watering eyes to see him smiling with satiated bliss.

With my free hand, I'd reach down and stroke myself. Stroking the way I am now, pulling and massaging my own man meat while imagining the sweet taste of Jarrod's dick in my throat.

"Let's cum together," I'd murmur with my mouth full of cock. He'd understand just what I was saying. Just what I was thinking. He always knows what I'm thinking, with his smart, smug smirk. The clever, cocky, condescending frat bro.

"Yeah, I want to." His voice would tremble, his labored breaths getting louder.

"I'm getting close," I hum to myself. I can feel the ache in my nuts, feel the sensations rising. "I'm almost there, Jarrod. Cum with me. Shoot your wad down my throat. Are you ready, Jarrod?"

"Not yet, but if you give me a minute to catch up..." his voice says with a stifled laugh.

It's then that I realize the voice isn't in my head. My eyes spring open and I turn around, swollen dick aimed like a gun in my hand, and find Jarrod standing on a rock just above me, peering down into the cave.

"Oh my god!" I stuff my frustrated cock back into my underwear and hastily fumble to find my zipper. "What are you doing here?"

"I think I could ask you the same. You were saying my name."

My face feels hot. I imagine it's as red as a tomato. "This isn't what it looks... I can't..." I sigh, realizing there's no way out of this. I throw my hands up in surrender. "Okay, you caught me. I was jacking off and imagining you."

I glare at him, expecting him to make some outrageous homophobic statement. Expecting him to berate and humiliate me. But instead, he just studies me, cold, calculating eyes sweeping over me, like he's trying to figure something out. What more could there be to figure out? All my secrets are laid bare now. "Aren't you going to say something?" I ask with exasperation.

"Do you want some privacy so you can finish?"

I stomp up the hill. "No, I don't want to finish. Jesus. You just caught me jacking off."

"So what?" The sound of Jarrod's footsteps trudge behind me. I briefly find humor in the fact that he's following me for once. "Ian, I have three brothers and we shared one bathroom. When guys live together, walking in on each other just comes with the territory. It's not a big deal. You should probably get used to it if you're gonna live in a house full of dudes."

I spin around to face him. "But I was saying *your* name."

"I told you I'm an open-minded guy. If thinking about me is what you've gotta do to get your rocks off, more power to ya. You think I work to have a body like this and expect people *not* to be fantasizing about me?"

I give him a once-over. He's put his shorts back on, but he's still shirtless. His confidence is infuriating. Even more maddening is how secure he is with his own sexuality. I shake my head. "I can't spend the night out here with you. Not after what you saw. Let's gather our stuff and hike back toward the main road. We can probably get a phone signal there."

Jarrod grabs me by the shoulder. It's the first time he's ever touched me. His hand is warm, strong and powerful as it grips me. "No fucking way. I'm not blowing our shot at joining this fraternity just because you were blowing your shot over me. You're gonna have to get over yourself. We're staying the night and that's final."

With that, the jock unhands me and takes off toward our campsite.

King Jarrod has spoken. All hail the hot ruler.

My nuts ache with unreleased tension and my cheeks burn with misplaced anger. I feel embarrassed, ashamed, and yet I have no one to blame but myself. It's going to be a long night, but it seems I have no choice. This is happening. I just hope I don't drown in my own desire.

CHAPTER 4

I unpack two turkey and cheese sandwiches from our mini cooler and hand one to Jarrod as if it's a peace offering. He unwraps the sandwich and sneers at it. "Does this have mayo on it?"

"Yeah, why?"

"Gross. I hate mayo." He takes a bird-like bite off the crust and chews it suspiciously.

"Geez, sorry," I say in a completely non-sorry tone. "You're acting like I served you a plate full of hot turds."

He unclenches his face and offers me a modest smile. "Sorry. That was rude of me. I guess I'm just hangry."

I throw him over a bag of chips. "Do you like Doritos?"

"Oh, hell yeah." He tears open the bag and starts crunching away at the reddish-orange triangles.

My phone chimes, reminding me to take our hourly selfie. I lean in and smile next to Jarrod, who grins with a mouth full of nacho cheesy crumbs while I snap the pic. When I tap the photo to review it, a billowy shadow in the background catches my eye. I swivel my head to see if it's still there, but I can't tell. My camera's night vision is better than my own.

"Hey, Jarrod, check this out." I zoom in to the shot and show him. "Do you see that?"

He squints at the image. "I dunno. Kinda."

"Do you think it could be a ghost?"

He rolls his eyes. "Probably."

"What?!"

"If ghosts exist here, they exist everywhere. Any time you've taken a photo in a park, or at the beach, or anywhere really, there were ghosts. Millions—*no, billions*—of people have died on this earth. There's nothing special about this place. I thought we already covered this."

His insistence on applying basic logic is maddening. "I guess you're right." I sigh and resume eating my mayo-licious sandwich.

Taking a softer tone, he adds, "This is a creepy place. I get it, bro. That's why we have to spend the night here. But I promise, it's going to be fine."

"Did you ever see *The Blair Witch Project*?"

"Dumb." He rolls his eyes and stuffs his perfect smirking lips with another handful of chips. "I wish there was a fire pit around here. It would be great to tell ghost stories around a crackling flame."

"That sounds terrifying. And dangerous."

Jarrod snorts. "C'mon, dude. We have all night. Let's kill some time. It'll be fun. Why don't you tell me which legend about these woods has you the most freaked out? When you say it out loud, I bet it won't even sound so scary."

I clear my throat and take a swig of water. "Okay. I guess it could be fun." I grab our battery-powered lantern and switch it on. It casts a wicked glow on Jarrod's face, illuminating him from below and casting large shadows above his eyes. "Damn, now you look creepy."

"Muhahaha." Jarrod makes a mock Dracula laugh and wiggles his cheesy fingertips at me.

"Alright, enough, enough." I take a seat on a tree stump and begin. "I think the creepiest story I've heard was about these two college students who camped out here one summer. During the night, this girl kept saying she heard this scratching sound on the outside of the tent. Her boyfriend said he didn't hear anything, and they both went back to sleep. In the middle of the night, the boyfriend got up to go pee. The girl heard him leave their tent, but she fell asleep again and didn't wake up again until morning. That's when she realized he hadn't returned to the tent. So she went outside to search for him. She found him slumped against a tree, dead. He'd been gutted with something. So she ran back to the tent and that's when she saw these long rips across the fabric in the roof. It was like someone had been trying to cut their way inside. She ran to the highway and got help. Well it turns out—"

"A psychopath escaped from the local prison, or asylum, or whatever, and he had a hook for a hand," Jarrod interrupts with a loud snicker.

I blink. "Yeah, that's the one. Did you hear about it too?"

He shakes his head, and now his whole body is convulsing with giggles. "Ian, Ian... Dude, are you really that gullible?"

I feel myself frowning like a petulant child. "What do you mean?"

"Do you know how many versions of that story exist? A man with a hook escapes from some sort of institution. The girlfriend hears a scratching sound, the boyfriend gets shredded, and later someone finds marks along the car, or house, or in this case, the tent. It's always the same legend, just a different setting."

"Well it could have happened," I insist.

"Are there any prisons within walking distance from here?"

I shake my head. "I don't know. I'd have to look it up."

"Spoiler alert: there aren't. We're thirty miles from town. Nobody built a prison or asylum out here in the middle of nowhere."

I chew my lip, tossing the story around in my head and feeling frustrated that I can't coax an explanation. It's then that I realize my hands are clenched so tight into fists that my knuckles are turning white. "Fine. I guess there's no way that could have happened."

"Don't be too hard on yourself, bud." Jarrod pats my shoulder. "I'm sure lots of people believe it happened."

I shrug his hand off me. "Your turn. Tell me a story you've heard."

Jarrod straightens his back. "Now, this one actually did happen. It was a night in September, kinda like this one. There was this guy named Tom, his wife, Rebecca, and their son, Matty, who was like four or five. I think five. They were out here camping. It was Matty's first time sleeping in the woods. He was really excited about it. They spent the day exploring, playing, whatever. That night, they're all asleep in the tent. Matty wakes up and Tom's not there. He wonders where his dad went, so he shuffles out of the tent and starts calling for him."

"And his mom's asleep through all of this?"

"Yes. It's just Matty. He's walking through the woods, and when he gets to the cave, he hears this horrible screaming sound. Like worse than he's ever heard in his life. It sounds like his dad's screaming bloody murder, and there's this banging sound too, like a fight's going on. Matty, being the brave little boy he is, runs into that cave to save his daddy. But he can't find him. He hears the screams, loud and clear, but he can't find where they're coming from. So Matty runs back to the tent to get his mom."

"I don't remember reading this story about the cave."

"It happened, okay? You can look it up when we get back home. Now stop interrupting me."

"Sorry."

Jarrod shoots me an annoyed glare but continues. "Rebecca grabs a flashlight and they take off toward the cave together. They both hear the screams. They're looking around, all over that cave, but they can't find Tom. They finally come to this super tight tunnel. It's really narrow. A grown man could never fit through it. A child could, maybe, but even that would be a real challenge. And that's where they hear the screams coming from. Clear as day. They try to see into the tunnel with the flashlight and there's this thrashing sound. Then they hear something getting slammed against the rocks. There's this thick, wet kind of gurgling sound. And the screams stop."

Jarrod clears his throat, takes a swig of water. He's trying to draw this out, really build the suspense. I hate the way his big, stupid lips purse when he thinks he's being clever. He's so self-assured, the dope. I'm dying to kiss him.

"Rebecca and Matty run to the highway searching for help. Thankfully a truck driver was passing by. They get the police out here, and there's no sign of Tom anywhere. A crew comes out and has to chisel and break their way into the rock to open up that tunnel. Inside, they find Tom's dead body. There's blood everywhere, big gashes all over him. They can't identify what did it. A bear, maybe, but the marks are way too big. And his throat has been sliced open. That's what that gurgling sound was. Rebecca and Matty heard Tom taking his last breaths."

"There was no other way into the tunnel?"

Jarrod shakes his head. "That tunnel had one way in and one way out. It led to a slightly larger area, but it was fully enclosed. The police figure somehow Tom crawled in and got cornered when an animal attacked. It's the only explanation that makes sense. But some people say the cave is haunted now. Tom's tortured soul lives there. And campers have sworn they heard Tom's blood-curdling screams coming from the cave in the middle of the night."

We sit in silence. The sun has disappeared and I can barely see the moon hidden above the dense cover of the trees. Darkness surrounds us.

"Well?" Jarrod finally asks, expecting some sort of reaction.

"That really happened out here?"

"I swear on my life." He raises his palm up and his other hand covers his heart. Once he's done gloating, he stops and stares at me, looking disappointed that I'm not scared.

Now it's my turn to burst into a fit of laughter. I don't know what's come over me. All the tension feels lifted from my shoulders as I double over.

"What's so funny, man?"

"You—" I can barely wheeze out my words. "You should see your face."

Jarrod furrows his brow, his face painted with confusion. Mr. Know-It-All is desperate to get the upper hand, but I can't stop laughing long enough to explain.

When I finally gain enough composure to offer an explanation, I wipe the tears from my eyes and try to keep a straight face. "You were just so committed to the story. You were so in it. Like you really wanted to scare the shit out of me. And it was good. It was *really* good. It made me realize what a wimp I've been about staying here."

A big grin fills the jock's face. Now we're both laughing hysterically, shoulders pressed together, just trying not to fall over.

"Okay, okay," I say finally. My stomach muscles burn, like I've just done a bunch of crunches. "I can't laugh anymore. I feel like I'm gonna die if I do."

Jarrod wipes at his eyes. "No, dude, don't die. Then you'll be part of the legend too."

All I can offer is a muted guffaw. I'm all laughed out. "Thanks, I needed that." I stand and head toward the tent. "I guess I'm gonna unroll my sleeping bag and try to get some rest. It's going to be a long night with us waking up to take selfies every hour. Might as well get some sleep when I can."

"Good idea," Jarrod agrees. "I'll get mine ready too."

It feels good to have shared a laugh with my roommate. I think all the mixed up feelings I have for him have made this camping trip twice as hard as it should have been. All we have to do is spend the night out here. It's not that much to do, really.

I'm still kind of embarrassed that he caught me jacking off while thinking about him. But he seems to be okay with it. I feel much better about the prospect of us sharing a room together. It's just dumb frat boy lust. Surely I'll get it out of my system and get over him.

Working by the light of the lantern, I unroll my sleeping bag while Jarrod does the same. At first, I'm confused. I stare at the flimsy piece of quilted polyester in my hands, then look at

Jarrod, and he looks at me. I feel around, turning the bag over, then flipping it around. I can't comprehend what I'm seeing.

Jarrod scowls. "What the hell, man?"

"No way."

I turn the bag over again. Turn it inside out, upside down. "Where's the lining? Where's the padding?"

It seems we reach the same conclusion at the same moment. "Chad," we say in unison. This must be the work of our chapter president. He's the only one evil enough to pull a prank like this.

Our sleeping bags aren't really bags at all. They've been modified, all of the stuffing removed and the seams stitched back into place. A single ply of silky material is all we were given. A roll of toilet paper would offer about as much warmth.

"How cold is it supposed to get tonight?"

"Down to the low '50s," I say.

"That's not...too bad, right?"

I check my phone. "Damn it. We still have ten hours to go. I guess we have to make the best of it. This isn't ideal, but it's not like we'll die."

Jarrod frowns. "The only person who's going to die this weekend is Chad."

CHAPTER 5

We make our best effort to get comfortable inside our sleeping bags, though it's a joke to even call them bags. The first few hours are filled with silence as we drift in and out of sleep. I don't normally go to bed this early, but when it's pitch black and all you're doing is lying there, it's kind of inevitable.

My phone chirps an annoying reminder every hour to take a selfie. Our efforts get sloppier, and by eleven, I'm merely holding the phone up over our heads, where we squint to avoid the blaring flash as I snap the picture. I don't bother checking if it's blurry or even if we're fully in the shot. Who the hell cares. I just want to make it through the night. Hopefully by this time in 24 hours, we'll join the initiation ceremony and then we'll be living it up at the fraternity's legendary fall party. I smile to myself as I imagine red Solo cups overflowing with beer.

Sometime after midnight, I wake up with a shudder. The temperature has drastically dropped, or at least it seems that way. Without Internet access, I can't be certain of exactly how cold it is outside. But the low '50s feel a lot colder without sunlight.

I roll over to my side and pull my knees to my chest. My movement stirs Jarrod, and then I hear his teeth chattering in my ear.

"F-f-fuck it's c-cold," he stutters.

I suck in a cold gulp of air. "Yeah."

"Do you...do you think we should—?"

I'm not sure what he's asking, so I roll over to face him. I can only see the outline of his face in the dim moonlight. "Think we should what?"

"We could try and warm each other up with our body heat."

"What do you mean?"

"Huddle together."

"Cuddle?"

"I said 'huddle,'" he says louder. "I'll press my body up against yours and we'll share the heat."

I'm suddenly stiff as a flagpole. "Uh, um, are you sure? Aren't you uncomfortable after earlier?"

"Dude, I'm freezing. And I already told you, it's not a big deal. Just..." He nudges me to roll over so he's facing my backside, then wraps his strong arms around me and spoons me tight against him. My breath catches in my chest. This has to be a dream. Or a trap.

But I'll take it. I lie in silence, feeling the steady rhythm of Jarrod's chest rise and fall against my back. His hot breath tickles my earlobe. And all the while, my cock is throbbing in my pants.

"Better?" I ask.

He nods against my shoulder. "I think we can make it through the night if we stay like this."

"I'll never let go, Jack," I say playfully.

"My name's Jarrod," he mumbles.

"It was a joke. You know, from *Titanic*."

"Never seen it."

"You've never seen *Titanic*?"

He cuddles closer. "Don't need to. I already know how it ends."

This guy is so pragmatic. I don't know why I'm attracted to him. But here we are, sandwiched together in the middle of the woods, while my dick throbs in my underwear and there's nothing I can do to soothe it.

Somehow I manage to fall asleep, and everything goes dark for a while, until I'm rustled awake again by the incessant alarm. I open one eyelid to see it's 2 AM. I don't recall taking a picture at 1 AM, but I don't even care. I aim the camera somewhere in the vicinity of my forehead, snap a selfie, and set my phone down.

I snuggle in tighter against Jarrod, and it's then that I realize something stiff is poking my bottom.

"Mmm, that felt good," he murmurs. I lie in silence, wondering if he's having a dream. He grabs hold of my waist and pulls himself tighter against me. "Do that again. Roll your hips."

"Jarrod, I think you're talking in your sleep," I whisper.

"I'm not asleep." His lips brush my ear. My whole body is covered in goosebumps.

I roll back against him, feeling his hard cock sink between my butt cheeks. He breathes against my neck, and I do it again. Then his hand grips me, and I know this is real.

"It's been so long," he says. "I haven't hooked up since Stacey dumped me last May."

"So you *are* straight?" I confirm.

"I'm hard is what I am," he mumbles impatiently. "Hard and horny and it's freezing out here."

"Do you think I could fit in your sleeping bag?"

The sound of him pulling down the zipper is the only answer I need. I slip out of my bag and into his. It's a tight fit. I'm pressed against his warmth and the soft flannel of his shirt. But something between us is remarkably hard.

"I bet it's warm in your mouth," he says.

"Let's find out." I slink down his torso, unfasten his shorts and pull them down just enough to get access. His balls feel heavy and warm as I roll them in my hand. He moans as I fondle him, stroking my fingertips up the length of his cock.

What Jarrod doesn't know, what I don't dare tell him, is that this is my first time with a guy. I don't know if I'll be any good at this, but I'm going to give it my best effort.

I shimmy further down in the bag until his throbbing rod is pressed against my face. It's warm and thick and his pubes tickle my nose. I swipe my tongue along his cock head, and he shivers. I never knew what a dick would taste like, but his tastes wonderful. I lick him again, fitting what I can into my mouth.

This feels so right as he slides across my tongue. His cock fills my mouth. I swipe the underside while breathing in the sexy scent of his manhood.

Something warm drips into the back of my throat. I swallow it down, and more fluid pulses out. His pre-cum tastes different than mine. Sweeter, and more potent. I swallow his juices down, feeling them run down my throat as I twirl my tongue up and down his shaft.

"You're really good at this," he says with a sigh. "Much better than any girl I've been with."

I beam with pride. That's high praise for a virgin like myself. Though I don't have any experience giving head, I know what feels good when I play with myself, so I just do what I think would feel good for him.

I squeeze him from the root, working my hand up and down while I get his cock nice and slick. That really seems to send him over the edge as he begins moaning louder and running his fingers through my hair.

"I bet your ass would feel so good," he says through jagged breaths.

I stop suddenly. "Really?"

"I mean...only if you'd be into that."

In the light of the moon, I can see his eyes bearing down on me. He's so dominant, so self-assured. In this new and unfamiliar territory, I still get the sense he knows exactly what to do, and exactly what he wants.

"We don't have any lube," I say.

"I'm a pretty heavy pre-cummer," he says. I feel a thick rope of fluid leaking down my hand, as if to prove his point.

"I've never done this," I confess.

"We can go slow." A barely visible smile pulls at his lips.

Feeling empowered, I roll my tongue across his sensitive cock head, taunting and teasing him. He lets out a long, low growl.

"Please, Ian, I want to fuck you so bad."

Gone is the cold that enveloped us. Gone is the shy virgin I once was. There's nothing left but red-hot passion now. I yank my shorts down to my knees. In a flash, I'm rolled over onto my stomach, offering my pure, untapped ass to Jarrod.

He hums with satisfaction as he climbs on top of me. I feel his weight, the hulking mountain of muscle as he takes control. Wasting no time, he slides his slippery cock between my cheeks. I feel my hole quivering with anticipation. It's all a feverish blur of horny frat boy heat.

He pushes his wet cock head against me. "I can already tell you're so fucking tight."

"Just go slow," I whimper.

He kisses the back of my neck to soothe me. Soft as the wings of a dove, a contrast to the rough graze of his chin stubble. But it does the trick, distracting me just long enough for him to start sliding the tip of his cock head past the gates of my resistance.

"Oh, god," I moan. His heavy balls brush against my thighs. He retreats, then thrusts forth once again. A little more of him squeezes inside me, and I relax as best I can.

"Just breathe." He reaches under my shirt, his fingertips surprisingly warm despite the temperature outside. He takes my nipple and gently rolls it between two fingers. A strange new tingle radiates through my chest. I've never played with my nipples before, and I love the way it feels.

My gasping breaths communicate that he's doing everything right. Emboldened, he gently twists and kneads my sensitive nip. His mouth finds its home on my ear, breathing softly against me, and his tongue traces the curve of my lobe. I shudder and squirm, so drunk with desire that I barely realize how deep he's slid inside me until I feel my tight virgin hole expand, gripping his cock like a well-fitted glove. And then the bulbous tip caresses something inside me that makes me feel like a hundred fireworks are blasting off all at once.

"Ahhh, Jarrod..."

He works his magic with playful fingertips and a talented tongue, sending chills down my spine as he stimulates all my erogenous zones. I want to touch myself so badly, but I'm held captive beneath him, unable to move as he thrusts his hard cock deep inside, then pulls it out to the tip.

I'm ready now. Relaxed and open, I settle in for the ride as he thrusts himself deep inside me once again. He pauses, as if seeking permission. "Yes," I hiss.

With that, he takes charge, pounding in and out of my tight hole. We're grunting and groaning together, a symphony of sensations, deep in the woods where no one can hear us, deep inside me, where no man has ever been.

Jarrod's breaths come long and quick, matching the rhythm of his hips, grinding in me with such force, I can hardly catch my breath. Each thrust presses against my swollen, sensitive sweet spot, sending sensations soaring. My cock is dripping against the sleeping bag, creating a slick friction each time the frat boy bangs into me.

"I think I'm close," Jarrod whispers.

"I think I am too."

He nips my ear, then twirls his tongue inside. That's all it takes to send me over the edge. As he thrusts himself inside me once more, hard and fast and impossibly deep, I clench my eyes shut and can swear I hear angels singing. My untouched cock pulses and tightens as I shoot my load all over my stomach.

"Ahhh, fuuuck," Jarrod moans as he explodes inside me. I squeeze my hole tight around his thick cock, determined to take every drop as he paints my insides with burning hot cum.

He keeps thrusting away, wild as an animal, wild as the way I feel for him, plunging so deep inside me and then pulling all the way out until just his tip is kissing the lips of my hole.

And once more, we crash together, until all the desire is drained from us.

When the thrusting stops and his hips are no longer pumping into me, I crane my neck back to look at the hot jock on top of me. "That was—"

"Incredible," he agrees, kissing me softly on the nape of my neck.

I don't understand how someone so tough can be so tender. One minute he is driving me mad with frustration. The next, he is driving me insane with desire. Jarrod is a perplexing puzzle that I can't wait to figure out.

Sandwiched together with his softening cock still buried inside me, Jarrod grabs my unused sleeping bag and pulls it over us like a blanket. Our breaths grow softer, our chests rising and falling in unison.

And then I hear the alarm trilling on my phone, nagging me to take our next selfie. I aimlessly tap away at the screen until I've opened the camera app, and then snap a blurry picture of the tent's roof. It will have to be good enough. And I am too happy to care.

Holding each other tight, Jarrod and I drift off to sleep.

CHAPTER 6

It's not the alarm that wakes me. It's the sound of screaming.

Loud and ricocheting through the forest, raining down on me like bullets.

I roll over to search for Jarrod, my hands grasping at the empty pile left from his sleeping bag. He's nowhere to be found.

The first thing that crosses my mind is the story he told. The cave. It was all a joke, right?

Then comes another scream, this one so piercing and deep from the person's lungs, there's no way they could be playing around.

I leap to my feet, my heart hammering in my ears. I'm wobbly and uncoordinated, my senses swimming, but I know I have to get my shoes on. I stumble around until I get them on my feet, then clutch the lantern and dart out into the darkness.

"Help me!" a man's voice screams. The terror in his trembling words is unmistakable.

I rush toward the sound, tripping over rocks and branches, fighting my way toward the cave with only the glow of the lantern to guide me. I can only see a few feet ahead of me, but I'm determined to make it.

I stop when I hit the water, watching it flow downstream like black ink. I tell myself I should turn back. Run to safety. But that voice, I'm so certain it's Jarrod's, and he needs me. I could never abandon someone in their time of need. It's not in my nature to run the other way.

One last scream echoes through the woods. It chills me to the bone. I snap my head toward the direction of the cave and rush to the battle zone.

It's dark inside as I make my way through the gaping maw of the rock.

"Hello?" I whisper into the nothingness. I don't know why I'm keeping my voice low. Sometimes when you're afraid, speaking louder feels even more terrifying.

"Ahhh!!!" is the response. A loud, desperate cry from deep within the cave.

The ground underneath me feels unsteady, a pathway formed from loose stones and wet debris. I scamper through it, guided by the lantern which swings back and forth in my hand.

I can't tell where I'm going, but only know that I'm getting further inside the cave, and the ceiling seems to come lower and lower until I find myself crouching down to walk.

"Jarrod, are you in here?" I call out to the shadows.

Just then, something grabs me by both arms and swings me around. My lantern crashes against the wall and shatters.

Something has a hold of me. It's squeezing me tight, holding me in place. And I can't see anything in front of me. All that's left to do is thrash and kick, trying to break free as I'm forced into this impossibly tight spot.

My mind races. Did I enter the tunnel without realizing it? Did I walk right into the space where that man died in Jarrod's story? Maybe it wasn't made up. Maybe this is how I die too. But I'm not going down without a fight.

I kick backwards, catching what feels like a leg behind me, and I pull it forward with my foot. The grip on my shoulders releases and whatever has a hold of me stumbles and falls to the ground.

"Alright, Ian, enough," a voice calls out breathlessly. "We're just messing with you."

A light appears, the flashlight of a cell phone. It takes a second for my eyes to adjust, and then I recognize the guy on the ground, covered in wet leaves and mud. "Chad?"

The prankster tries to laugh, but it comes out as a cough. "Fuck. Yeah, it's me. You really knocked the shit out of me."

The sound of hands clapping echoes from somewhere in the darkness. I spin around to see another cell phone flashlight floating near me. It's Jarrod, a satisfied grin filling his face.

I help Chad up from the ground. He wipes himself off and then pats me on the back.

"No one's ever come to the cave," he says.

"What do you mean?"

"Beta Gamma Zeta has been pulling this prank for almost twenty years. It's a longstanding tradition. Every single recruit has gone running up the hill toward the highway. You're the first one who's run to the cave trying to be a hero."

"You must have a brave heart," Jarrod adds, wrapping his arm around my shoulder and giving me a squeeze.

"You knew about this?"

He shrugs impishly. "I mean, yeah. Like I said earlier, I've been hanging out with these guys since tenth grade." Then he turns to Chad with a glare. "What I didn't know about was the unlined sleeping bags."

Chad laughs. "That's a new twist on the tradition. I thought of it myself."

"It was brutal." I know I should be more upset, but I can't stop smiling. "Please tell me we've passed the test. I don't want to go back to that cold tent."

"You can sleep here in the cave instead," Chad offers.

"Forget that." Jarrod takes me by the arm and leads me out of the cave. "We've more than proven our worth to join the fraternity. And Ian here has proven he's got bigger balls than any one of us." He leans close to whisper in my ear, "And I should know."

His warm breath on my neck makes me shudder, thinking about our secret sex.

Chad follows behind us. "Alright, boys, let's head home."

"I can't wait to get back to a warm bed," I say with relief.

Jarrod nudges me as we walk. Just knowing he'll be sleeping on the other side of our room sends me reeling with filthy fantasies.

I look over at him and catch his eyes gleaming under the moonlight. From the way he's looking at me, all hot and bothered with lust in his stare, I think it's safe to say I'm not the only one imagining the next time we hook up.

He winks at me, and then I know for sure. This is the beginning of something wonderful.

SEDUCED BY THE

NEIGHBOR

CHAPTER 1

It's early morning and I'm lost in a dream, somewhere in the realm where consciousness and unconsciousness blend.

A stranger touches me with velvet hands. A mystery, a blur, someone I can't identify, but I feel their touch as they caress my thigh. I shudder. My cock is rock hard and throbbing.

"Let's go higher," they murmur.

I don't know what that means, but I'll follow them anywhere.

We move through the air. Are we climbing? Floating? Suddenly we're on a cliff, peering down at the world below.

This dream lover claims me with their lips. A shadow in the light. I can't see their face, but I feel their mouth as our kiss deepens. It's like every touch is hardwired to the ache between my legs. The slightest brush of their hand could make me cum.

I feel myself closer to the edge. There's a stirring in my balls. I'm so close to the feeling. So close, but then I fall...

Flying.

No, dropping.

Crashing.

Hurling into the dark abyss.

I'm startled awake.

The sweetest dream turned into a nightmare in an instant. I'm covered in sweat and my chest is heaving. My bedroom is sweltering.

Damn it, the air conditioner must be on the fritz again. The thing is ancient and barely cools my room on the second floor. I always have weird dreams when I get too hot.

I try to shake it off, this strange groggy feeling somewhere between horny and horrified. I check my phone. It's 8:35 AM. For me, that's sleeping in. I usually get up around 6:30. It's nice to be a little lazy.

This is the first day of summer break and I have no plans for anything except relaxation. I've just survived my freshman year of college. Final exams kicked my ass hard. Thankfully I finished strong. Now I need some time to unwind.

Most of my housemates left town last night. They have family within driving distance. Mine is eight hundred miles away. The cost of travel right now is outrageous and I couldn't swing a ticket, so I told my parents I'd check for deals closer to autumn.

I scroll through my phone. There's a package delivery notification. My new Nintendo Switch Pro game controller was dropped off a few minutes ago. Hell yeah.

I fling off the covers and rush downstairs wearing just my boxer briefs. I still have half a chub and it's swinging like mad, but I'll be back to my room in a flash.

Sunlight is bursting through the windows that frame the door. It's a little too bright for first thing in the morning. I shield my face as I open the door, and I'm startled to find a man standing at the doormat, his hands on his hips and a deep crease between his eyebrows. He towers over me like a mountain of muscle. His baby blue button-up hugs his shoulders like it's painted on.

I gasp and step back. "Shit, you scared me."

His eyes flick across my exposed torso, and I'm sure he can see the outline of my cock. Now I really regret not getting dressed.

"Where's John?" the man asks. There's an edge to his voice.

"John Davis or John Miller?" I ask.

The man sighs. "I don't know. The blond one."

"They both have blond hair."

"Okay, well which one is home?"

"They're both gone."

"Great. I don't have time for this. I should have been on the road fifteen minutes ago."

I look down at the padded envelope. It's only inches from the guy's feet. I'm seriously contemplating swiping the package and slamming the door shut. This isn't my problem. All I want to do is dump a box of Cocoa Krispies into a mixing bowl and chow down while playing Nintendo.

"Can you do me a favor and try calling both of them?" The man's eyes soften. "Please? Maybe they'll answer if you call. Then we can sort this out."

I close the door halfway and lean against the back of it. "Look, mister, I don't even know what this is about."

The man's face flushes pink. He pinches the bridge in his nose and exhales loudly. "I'm going to the beach for the weekend. John's supposed to housesit while I'm gone. He said it was no problem."

Then something clicks into place and I remember where I've seen this guy. "Oh, right, you're the dude who lives behind us."

The man nods. "Yeah, I'm that 'dude.'"

"Then you must be talking about John Miller. John Davis would never agree to help someone."

"Good, okay, now we're getting somewhere. Can you call John Miller from your phone? He's not picking up when I call."

I suck in air through my teeth. "Look, that wouldn't do any good. John went to the beach for the weekend with his girlfriend."

"What?!" A vein pulses in the man's forehead.

"Yeah, um, that's John for you. He means well, but he spaces out like all the time. He probably just forgot."

The man shakes his head. "Great. Just great. So John gets to enjoy the beach and I have to cancel on my friends and stay home."

I choke back a laugh and say, "A guy your age still goes to the beach with his friends?"

The man's blue eyes turn to ice. "Yes, a guy my age still goes to the beach with his friends. I'm 42, not 92."

"I'm so sorry." I hold my hands up defensively. "I just woke up and came out here to grab that package by your feet. I haven't had any coffee yet and I'm not thinking straight."

The man picks up the envelope and hands it to me. "No, I'm sorry. This isn't your fault. I shouldn't be taking it out on you. Thanks for letting me know about John."

As I watch my neighbor stomp away, my hazy brain finally puts two and two together. "Hey, wait. Were you paying John to housesit?"

The man turns around and nods. "Yeah. Fifty bucks a day to feed my cat and water my plants."

"How many days?"

"Three. Are you interested?"

"I think so." I step out from the door, forgetting I'm half naked until the man's eyes wash over my bare skin again.

"You're not going to run off with your girlfriend, are you?"

I laugh and wave away the thought. "Not a chance."

"Alright," the man says, "that would be great. Wanna get dressed and meet me over at my house?"

I feel the heat crawl up my cheeks as I cover my protruding cock with the envelope. "Yeah, I'll be over there in five minutes."

He nods. "See you soon."

I rush back into the house and up the stairs to grab a pair of sweatpants and t-shirt from my bed. On the way out, I stop in the kitchen to turn on the coffee machine so I'll have a fresh cup waiting for me. Two of my housemates, Cole and David, are sitting at the table.

"Hey, Lance," Cole says to me. "What was that all about?"

"Apparently John Miller skipped town after promising to housesit for the neighbor behind us. I offered to do the job instead."

"Are you talking about our neighbor Edward?"

I shrug, suddenly feeling dumb for not asking the guy's name. "I guess. The house right there." I nod toward the window at the partial view of a small Craftsman-style home.

Cole and David exchange glances. David snickers. "You know that guy's gay, right?"

Something stirs deep inside me. "No, um... I didn't. But who cares? A job's a job."

"Yeah, well be careful over there. He'll probably offer you a different kind of job."

I shake my head. "You guys are being stupid. It's none of our business. All I'm doing is feeding his cat and watering the plants."

"Alright, whatever, man," David concedes. "Just don't bend over in front of him. He might pop your butt cherry."

I feel my cock start to plump. Something is definitely going on with me today. Maybe I'm still worked up about the dream I had.

"I'll be back soon," I say, ignoring their jokes. "I just got the new Switch Pro controller if you want to play Mario Kart with me."

"Sorry, can't," Cole says. "While you're over there hanging out with that old homo we're meeting up with some friends for lunch. And then tonight we're going to a big summer bash. You should join us."

I shake my head. "Maybe another time. You guys have fun."

As I head out the back door to cut through our yard, my heart races. Suddenly I'm nervous. I don't know why. Who cares if our neighbor is into dudes? It's not like I'm gay.

CHAPTER 2

The front door swings open before I knock, sending cool air against my face. "Come in," Edward says.

"Nice place," I say, checking out the entryway foyer. The walls are painted a warm brown tone with a finish that resembles aged leather. As I step inside, my nose is filled with something fresh and spicy. "God, it smells good in here. Is that air freshener?"

"No, it's my cologne." A smile spreads on my neighbor's face. "Probably smells a lot different over here than in your frat house."

"Stale beer and sweaty jockstraps," I agree with a nod.

Edward shrugs his round shoulder. "Jockstraps aren't so bad," he says with a curl in his lip.

I laugh nervously, uncertain why I'm feeling a strange tingle in my stomach. "I guess not."

The house feels so refreshing. It's nice to be in a place with real air conditioning to wick away the humid summer heat from my skin.

My eyes are drawn to a large framed painting on display above a half-moon shaped console table. I move closer to examine it.

"Are you a fan of George Quaintance's work?" Edward asks.

The art features two men with glistening muscles, facing one another beside a pool. On the left is a man who's nearly nude. His dense thatch of black pubic hair plays peek-a-boo behind his towel, offering only a hint of what's hidden beneath. Beside him is a blond, also nude, turned inward. The blond seems to be revealing himself, but I, the voyeuristic audience, am left with only my imagination.

I suddenly realize Edward asked me a question and it's taken me waaay too long to respond. My cheeks flush hot. "Are these guys gay?" I ask.

There's a glimmer in Edward's eyes. "Does it matter?"

Everything the man says is a mystery. He hints at something dirty, something secret, but he never comes out with it.

"No." I shake my head. "Just curious."

"Nothing wrong with curious." Edward flashes me another sly grin. "Anyway, I was saying George Quaintance is the artist. The piece is called 'Spartan Soldiers Bathing.' Now if you don't mind, I really do need to get going."

"Oh, right." I chuckle and run my hand across the back of my neck. "So, where's your cat?"

"Hiding. You probably won't see him." Edward nods toward the main living area. I follow behind him, sneaking a quick peek at the furniture. Everything is decorated in dark earth tones and silver accents. His sleek couch is brown leather, probably real leather, I imagine. His home feels so masculine and mature, refined.

We breeze through the kitchen and stop in the connected laundry room. A single window with drawn blinds allows the sun to bathe the space in natural light.

"Do you know how to scoop litter?" Edward nods at the box in the corner by the dryer.

"Yep," I nod. "I grew up with several pet cats."

"Good. Once a day is fine." We drift back into the kitchen and walk to the other side where two bowls sit by the breakfast bar. One is filled with water, the other with dry kibble. "Please refill his food bowl in the morning. He won't finish it, but that's okay. I like food to be available just in case. Refill his water bowl with fresh water, too."

"That's easy enough," I remark.

Edward raises his eyebrow. "You'd think so, right? I really didn't ask John for much."

I snort. "How did you and John ever get mixed up anyway? He's like the least responsible person I know."

"Clearly." Edward sighs. "I caught him lounging in my hammock a few nights ago. He had his feet up, a joint between his fingers, acting like he owned the place. When I first smelled it, I thought I had a skunk in my backyard. With a frat house next door, I never know for sure."

I stifle a laugh. "Ah, I see."

"I honestly don't care what you boys do," Edward says, sounding very fatherly all of a sudden. "But I don't appreciate people trespassing on my property."

"Of course not," I say agreeably.

"At first John gave me a lot of attitude, saying I was overreacting. But then he changed his tune when I told him I was calling the cops. He said he'd do anything to make it up to me. I was already in a bind because my regular house sitter injured her ankle and is on bed rest for the next few days. So I figured having a neighbor help out would be the perfect arrangement. John and I exchanged numbers. I texted him last night to confirm we were still on, and he wrote back yes."

I shake my head. "John was already at the beach last night."

"That little punk."

"Yeah, that's John." I chuckle. "If you don't mind my asking, why'd you buy a place next to a frat house anyway? Our house can get pretty noisy, and uh, kinda skunky."

"I didn't buy a place next to a frat house," Edward says pointedly. "This is one of the original houses on the block, built in 1943. It's been in my family for five generations. The university bought your place and converted it into a frat house in the '90s. It's been a nuisance ever since. I could probably make half a million selling my place today, but nobody wants to buy a house next to a fraternity."

"Oh. Got it." I smile sheepishly. "So, uh, your plants?"

Edward nods toward the living room. A fern hangs by the window, and there are several potted plants throughout the room. "I've already watered them for today. Give them a little water in the morning. There are also a few plants in my bedroom and bathroom."

That same strange stirring takes over as I follow behind Edward to the sunlit room at the end of the hallway. I watch the way he moves. There's a confident glide to his gate, smooth with a feline prowess. He keeps his head high, his shoulders back and chest out.

"The palm doesn't need any water," he says, looking toward the potted tree by the bedroom window. "Just the ones in the bathroom."

We step into the oversized bathroom suite, which looks newly renovated with smooth granite countertops in earth tones. "A little water for that one," he says, pointing up to a viny plant that hangs from a ceiling basket. "And that one is fine." He tilts his head toward the small succulent in the window sill.

I give the place a quick once-over, and that's when my eyes wander back toward the bedroom, where a long black device sits on his night table, cradled in a charger. It has a futuristic design, like some sort of joystick. I wonder if it's a high-tech game controller.

"Wow, what's that?" I shuffle into the bedroom to get a closer peek.

Edward sweeps up beside me, snatches the device from its dock and stuffs it into a drawer. "It's a stress reliever," he says, clearing his throat.

Then it all comes together in a flash. The flared base, the bulbous tip. I suddenly realize it's a sex toy. "Sorry," I say, feeling my cheeks getting hot.

"No worries." Edward claps his hands together. "If that's everything, I think I'll head out."

"Yep, everything makes sense."

We exchange numbers and I agree to give him an update tonight. "It probably goes without saying," he adds with a stern look in his eyes, "but don't throw any parties here and don't bring any guests over while I'm gone."

"Definitely not," I agree. And because it somehow feels warranted, I add, "Sir."

Edward smiles approvingly. "Good, I'm glad we're on the same page. Thanks for doing this for me."

"Any time," I say, with a strange lilt in my voice. "I mean, whatever, dude," I add, lowering my voice an octave.

God, what is going on with me today?

I follow Edward out toward the front door. As we pass the foyer, I can't help throwing another glance at the artwork on the wall. It's just a fraction of a second, but Edward catches me. His blue eyes sparkle.

"George Quaintance," he reminds me. "I have a book of his artwork on the shelf behind the couch if you'd like to explore your curiosity further. Just please don't get anything on the pages. It's a very rare, out of print copy."

"Oh, um, no," I say, shaking my head and making some sort of weird huffing noise. "I mean..." Then I shake my head again and wave my hand dismissively. "I was just looking."

"Which is why I offered to let you check out the book." Edward smiles like it's obvious.

We walk out to the porch, he locks the door behind us and hands me the key. "Oh, hey, what's your cat's name?" I ask.

"Mouse."

"Mouse, the cat?" I ask.

"Mouse, as in Michael Tolliver." He smirks. "Mouse is a character in one of my favorite books."

"Oh."

"There's a lot I could teach you," he says.

"I'm sure you could." There it is again, that strange, flirty lilt in my voice that makes it sound like I'm delivering a line. I stuff my hands toward my sides, forgetting my stupid sweatpants don't have any pockets. Instead, I just brush my slippery palms down my lap and have no way to come back from my humiliation.

Edward smiles, unflinching to my clumsy awkwardness. "See you later."

"Uh-huh, yup." I deliver my final cringe-inducing blow by raising my hand to my forehead and making a saluting gesture.

I just want to crawl into a hole and die.

CHAPTER 3

I spend the rest of the day up in my room trying to ignore how hot and bothered I felt in the presence of Edward. Playing games with my new game controller provides a momentary distraction, but my mind keeps wandering to him.

Outside my bedroom window, I can see Edward's side yard. It's partially obstructed by trees and a brick wall that's overgrown with ivy. I can only see a little through the leaves. Then it dawns on me that my phone makes a better telescope than my eyes.

I open the camera app and focus on the bare spots between the vines. When I zoom in, I find a pair of frosted windows. That must be his bathroom. Following my line of sight, I see white curtains that are partially drawn. On the window sill sits Mouse, the cat. He's the color of dark ashes, curled up with his eyes closed, napping in the sun.

Just behind Mouse must be Edward's bed. I think of the smooth 'stress reliever' gadget I saw on his nightstand and feel curiosity stirring.

Damn, what's going on with me?

I don't know why, but I want to go over and explore. I try to hold off. It takes all my self control to make it until five o'clock. By then, I figure it's justifiable to go over. Edward told me to check in tonight.

I've showered but I'm still in my usual loungewear. The day grew even hotter so I've changed from my sweatpants to a clean pair of basketball shorts and a comfortable tank top. I slip on some sandals and head downstairs.

Cole and David are in the foyer getting ready to head out. They've cleaned up and look surprisingly decent.

"You sure you don't want to come with?" Cole asks.

"Nah, I'm about to head over and check on the neighbor's cat."

"How long does that take, five minutes?" David says. "C'mon, we can wait for you. Check on the cat, change your clothes, and we'll head out."

The thought of going to a loud beer bash doesn't appeal to me. Besides, I really want to spend some time snooping at Edward's place.

"I'm good, thanks," I say. "I just wanna play video games and relax."

Cole shakes his head. "Suit yourself. More pussy for us."

We walk out together and part ways. I cut through our yard and walk up to Edward's porch. Once again, there are butterflies in my stomach. I feel like I'm breaking the law. But he gave me the key. I'm just doing what he asked me to do. What he's paying me to do.

I insert the key into the lock. As it turns, I feel my heart leap. I open the door and am overcome once again with the invigorating fragrance of Edward. Cool air tickles the hairs on my arms, causing goosebumps to form on my skin.

In here, everything smells so good, feels so cool and relaxing. I get a strange mix of contentment infused with pure adrenaline as I shut the door behind me. I look around suspiciously, like I expect Edward to pop out at any second.

"Hello?" I call out.

Stupid, I know, but it helps assure my hammering heart that I'm truly alone.

With nobody around to cast questioning glances my way, I finally feel free to explore the art on the foyer wall.

Although the painting is a poster print, the detail is still very sharp. I can see the raw beauty of the brush strokes, admire the way the light accentuates the men's bodies, the way water drips off their skin.

There's so much unspoken lust and longing between them. It's palpable. I can't help but feel teased, yearning to see what's hidden out of view.

In the background, more action takes place. There are men in the pool, naked, of course, but their lower bodies are obscured. Another man sits on the edge, watching... Waiting, maybe. And in the corner, there are two more pairs of men, each of them engaged in conversation that makes me curious.

It's like porn, except it's not porn at all. There are so many ways to interpret the scene. I don't know if I'm reading too much into it, and I don't understand why it makes me feel drunk with desire wishing I could live inside that world.

Just as I feel myself getting too hot to tame, the air conditioner kicks on, blowing crisp air from the vent above me. My nipples harden to stiff peaks, sensitive and tender against the thin fabric of my shirt. I shudder and fold my arms across my chest. I'm starting to feel sensory overload.

I move deeper into Edward's home, tiptoeing with caution. I still feel like an intruder. The scent of him lingers. It's like he permeates the air I breathe, and his fragrance lures me toward the back hallway, where it intensifies.

The door to his bedroom is open. It's darker in there. The sun is setting behind the trees and now it glows beyond his curtains in golden shards.

"Here, kitty, kitty," I say. "Mouse, where are you?"

I really don't care either way. Edward said his cat would probably hide, so I don't expect to find him. But calling the feline's name makes me feel less creepy as I edge closer to the bedroom at the back of the house.

"Here, Mouse. Come on out."

My sandals pad softly on the cream-colored carpet. I make my way to the doorway and stop. The bedroom curtain spreads in the middle, just open a bit. It's the same window I saw Mouse sleeping in from my house.

There's a rustle under the bed. I know the cat is hiding underneath. I crouch down and peek beneath the wood frame. Two yellow eyes shine back at me, large and alert.

"Hey, bud," I say, slowly extending my hand so he can inspect me.

Mouse tentatively sniffs my fingertips. I stay still, not making any sudden moves.

He seems neither pleased nor displeased as he resumes staring at me. That's okay. I know cats prefer to be left alone until they feel comfortable with a stranger.

It's then that I spot something balled up behind the back corner of the bed. Curious, I reach under and pull it out for a closer look.

I realize it's a jockstrap. Maybe some discarded laundry that fell behind the bed when Edward was folding it.

I recall the alluring way he said to me, "Jockstraps aren't so bad." Like a playful nudge, seared into my memory.

Curiosity consumes me, so I raise the jockstrap to my nose and take a deep inhale. The funk fills my nostrils, familiar and yet foreign. It's earthy with a slightly sweaty tang. This isn't clean laundry, I realize. It's been worn.

I can't believe I'm holding another dude's dirty underwear in my hand. But I'm not grossed out. Not like I thought I would be. There's something virile to its aroma. An extension of Edward's commanding presence.

The room is spinning. I sit on the bed to gather my thoughts. The air is thick with Edward's cologne and now my hand is stained with his sweat. My eyes flick to the nightstand. Inside the drawer is his toy. His *sex* toy. Yes, I know what I saw. He called it a stress reliever. I find myself wondering if it would ease some of the strange tension I've been feeling today.

I take hold of the drawer handle. Its cold metal burns against my skin. This is forbidden. I shouldn't be doing this. And yet...

The drawer slides open. There's the toy, resting on top of a bottle of lube.

I pick up the toy—the stress reliever. It's thick and heavy in my hand. Smooth black material that glistens in the low light. Glistens, just like the models in that painting. Glistens just like a fresh load of hot, sticky—

My phone vibrates against my leg. I drop the toy back in the drawer like it's on fire. The caller ID shows it's Edward.

"Hey," I answer, trying to steady my breath.

"Hey, Lance," he says. There's music in the background and the sound of people talking and laughing. "I'm just touching base. Have you had a chance to go over and check on Mouse yet?"

"Yeah, um, I'm actually over at your place now."

"Good. Any signs of the little guy?"

"I found him under your bed. He gave me a sniff, but that's it."

Edward chuckles, low and deep in his chest. "That means he likes you."

"It does?"

"He didn't run away?"

"No."

"Consider it a compliment," Edward assures me.

"Oh. Uh, thanks."

"Well, listen, I really appreciate you helping me out when I was in a bind. I'm sorry for being rude to you earlier. None of this was your fault."

"Hey, no problem. It's easy money. How's the beach?"

I listen to him sigh happily. "Just what I needed. There's a band playing on the pier. I'm having drinks with my friends. Couldn't ask for a better day."

"Good, I'm glad."

"I won't keep you," Edward says. "Just wanted to check in. Let me know if anything pops up."

I look down at the relentless tent I've pitched in my shorts. "Sure, I'll do that."

The call ends. I lie down, making myself comfortable. I can smell him on the pillow just as if he were in the bed with me.

My cock twitches, painfully hard and desperate for relief. I look over the edge of the drawer. Curiosity overwhelms me.

A stress reliever is just what I need right now.

My heart feels like it's in my throat as I reach for the toy. Picking it up, I feel its weight in my hand, wrap my fingers around its girth.

Devious, dirty thoughts stir in my head.

Nobody will ever know.

It can be my little secret...

I hold Edward's dirty jockstrap in my hand, raise the balled up treasure to my nose once again. This time, I smell it with purpose, taking a deep, heavy whiff.

Damn, he smells incredible...

I pull back the sheets, get comfortable in his bed. As I tug off my shorts, a zing of nervous energy races up my spine.

This is so bad.

So very, very bad.

And yet, as I free my desperate cock, all fear disappears. My foreskin's drawn back tight as a drum, the crown burning bright pink.

I take another hit off the jock. It's like a drug. I'm high on the scent of a man's balls. I can't believe it, but I won't deny it.

I grab the bottle of lube, pop open the lid, and pour it onto my fingers. It spreads like liquid silk between my fingertips. I reach behind me and spread it across my tight pucker.

Another burst of excitement ripples through me. I've never touched myself like this. I give a gentle push against my hole, feel the tight band of muscle. There's resistance at first. A strange and foreign sensation. But as I push a little firmer, my hole spreads open like lips. Soft and tender, the virgin flesh kisses my fingertip. A little 'hello,' welcoming me inside.

I turn my attention to the sex toy. Its bulbous head is smooth and round at the tip. Another hit from Edward's underwear to calm my nerves.

Ahhh... That's better.

I drizzle a thick load of lube all over the toy, watch as the crystal clear fluid drips down the sides of the shaft. I hold it in my hand like a magic wand, and aim it toward my tight hole. Not sure what to expect, I apply gentle pressure between my ass cheeks.

Fuuuck...

It's like nothing I've ever felt before, a surge of electric current that starts deep between my legs and spreads all through me. The sensation is better than anything I've felt stroking my dick. Has my hole been the secret gateway to paradise all along?

There's tension as I try to ease the head inside me. My hole clenches. I wiggle the toy and gently prod it upward. At once, my muscles relax. A barrier is broken, I feel myself open up and the thick tip slides inside.

Oh, my god. It's Christmas, my birthday, and the Fourth of July all rolled into one, like a fireworks explosion inside me. It burns and aches, yet tingles so nicely. I hold back and take a deep breath, let my body adjust to the new guest.

Another hit off the deepest crevice of Edward's jockstrap, then I adjust the grip on the toy and push it inside me once more. This time it slides a little easier. The ache has dulled to a whisper. Like a greedy savage, my body pulls the shaft inside me. My finger flicks against a button on the bottom. A button I didn't notice. And then the toy buzzes to life.

My new best friend, the stress reliever purrs like a kitten, pulsing sonar waves all through my insides. My eyes roll back in my head, I bite my lip and out rolls a deep sigh of ecstasy. I push the button again, and the humming intensifies.

With my legs spread, I settle onto my back and get comfortable. I hold the toy in my right hand and slowly begin working it in and out of my hole. With my free hand, I spread the jock across my nose and mouth, letting its potent aroma fill my nostrils. The virile scent of Edward consumes me.

I drive the toy deep inside me. It rattles and shakes me to my core. Then its round head slides like a fat tongue against my inner walls, and I'm taken to a new level of ecstasy. I don't know what I just hit, but it's like a switch inside me has been activated.

I retreat, pulling the toy back slightly, then push it once again toward this special spot. My nipples harden, and I feel a shudder all through me.

This time, I hold the toy in place, the thick head against this sensitive area. It rumbles against me. My cock weeps tears of joy. I've never felt this good in my life.

My entire body's humming. Something sings deep behind my balls. I take a long hit off my neighbor's underwear. I'm not even touching my cock but I can feel a climax soaring to the surface.

I push harder with the toy, angle it just right so the vibrations pulse against the magic spot. My quivering fingers brush against the bottom on the toy and crank up the vibrations to level three.

Ohhhmyyyygoddd!!!

The floodgates open. My cock shoots missiles of thick, hot cum in the sky. They land on my skin, one after another, I paint myself with my seed.

When I've finally pulsed all the lust out of me, I lift the underwear from my face, scrunch it together in my hand. I can smell my hot neighbor all over my face. He's all around me like a ghost, the aroma of him mingles with the scent of my release.

I've never felt this way about a man before. I've never felt this way about anyone, really. I know I need to get back home, get some air, and give myself a little space from a man who makes me weak with desire.

I need to get my head on straight.

CHAPTER 4

The next morning, I wake up to the sound of raindrops against my window. It's Sunday, and I feel like my whole world has been turned upside down.

Last night when I got home, I tried to get the fantasy out of my head. But all I could think about was taking things further. I want more than a toy and a sweaty jockstrap. I think I want to experience the real thing.

I noticed one of my frat brothers getting out of the shower. His body was wet and gleaming, just like a guy in that painting. The sight of him caused a stirring inside me. Something new is awake.

Imagine a picture taken on an overcast day. It's not a very interesting picture, the colors are muddy and dull. But you start playing around with filters on that picture. You amp up the contrast, send the saturation through the roof. Now everything is vivid and bright. You see details in that picture differently now. It's the same scene, but everything has changed. That's a metaphor for my life.

I think about how closed off I've been. I was never too interested in much of anything or anyone other than video games. And I think about a world of possibilities where I can feel as good as I felt last night.

Too excited to bother with breakfast, I pull on some clothes and head back to Edward's house. I tell myself I'm just doing my job. I need to feed the cat, clean the litter box, water the plants. But as my heart thuds in my chest with each step closer I get to his front porch, I know what I really want.

That big, hard toy. That feeling inside me as I ride the wave. It's perverse and feels so wrong, but I'm greedy and desperate to feel it again.

Mouse, the cat, is hiding from me. No surprise there. I fill his food bowl, give him fresh drinking water, and clean his litter box. The plants look happy. I mist the fern and add a little water to the potted plants, just as Edward instructed me.

All done.

I step into Edward's bedroom, cautiously approaching his bedside table as if a bomb is waiting to go off. I know I shouldn't be doing this, but I can't help myself.

My hands tremble, my fingers twitchy and uncoordinated as I slide open the drawer. Though it's raining out, a ray of daylight cuts through the curtains. Seeing the object of my desire in brighter light makes the moment feel all the more real and dangerous.

I look behind me. No one's around. Obviously. Between shaky breaths, I grab hold of the sleek shaft, feel its strength in the palm of my hand. It's smooth like satin, but hefty, too.

There's no time to waste. No turning back now. I fling off my shorts. I didn't even bother putting on underwear before I left my house. And in a flash, I'm on top of Edward's bed, my knees bent as I straddle the beast. I grab the bottle of lube from the drawer, pop open the lid and drizzle it all over the toy.

My body tightens with anticipation as I bring the smooth head to my hole. They kiss, long and wet, the toy already pushing its way inside.

I feel myself pucker, my muscles spasm. It's only the second time in my life that I've been seized this way. I push through my resistance, desperate to be filled.

And just like yesterday, there's a tense moment where everything feels unbearably tight, immediately followed by the relief as a barrier is breached. I've managed to push the long shaft through my body's resistance, and now it fills me to the hilt.

With a jagged sigh, I relax and settle down onto the toy, taking it all the way to its flared base. And then I rise up again. It strokes against me, touching me in all the right ways.

Damn, it feels so incredible...

I start riding the toy, close my eyes and imagining it's Edward under me. I'm not shy anymore, allowing myself to surrender to the fantasy.

I imagine his strong chest flexing with each breath. His cool blue eyes watch me as I ride him.

I bite my lip. "You feel so good, Edward" I murmur.

"I'm glad you're enjoying yourself," he says in a low growl.

But wait...

My eyes fly open. I turn toward the bedroom doorway, my mouth drops with surprise.

Edward is standing there, in the flesh, his excitement is evident by the massive bulge pulling at the front of his shorts. He appraises me with a wicked grin.

"Oh, my god! Edward!" I quickly unmount from the sex toy and leap off the bed, covering myself with my hands.

"So this is what you do when I trust you alone in my house?" He circles the bed, filling the space between us.

"I'm so, so sorry." My face is burning hot. My eyes flick to the toy on the bed. He looks at it, then at me. And he smiles.

"I didn't know you had it in you," he says playfully.

"What are you doing home early?"

"I called you two times and sent you a text."

"I must have missed those," I lie.

The truth is, I didn't even check my phone when I got up this morning. I was so excited to get over here.

"That's alright." Edward peers out the window. "It's raining. The beach is no fun in the rain. And it's supposed to rain the rest of the week. Bummer because rain wasn't in the forecast. I guess Mother Nature conspired to get me home early."

"I can explain," I offer clumsily.

Edward crosses his arms. His biceps pop as he holds them taut against his chest. "Oh?"

"This isn't what it looks like."

He smiles with amusement. "I really don't see how that's possible."

"Okay, well it is what it looks like. I just got so curious."

"As I said yesterday, there's nothing wrong with curious."

"Right." I clear my throat.

"You could have put a towel down first," he says, eyeing the big spot of lube I've left on his bed.

"Oh, I'm so sorry." I grab hold of his sheets and begin stripping his bed. "I can throw these in the laundry for you."

"Lance, take a breath." Edward puts his hands on my shoulders.

I shudder under the warmth of his touch. My eyes meet his. "Are you going to call the cops?"

Edward laughs gently. "And tell them what? 'Oh, hello, officer, I caught my house sitter fucking himself in my bed.'" He switches voices and speaks out one side of his mouth, imitating some old-timey caricature of a cop. "'Take him away, boys.'"

I feel my cheeks turn red with blush. "So you're not mad?"

"Mad? It isn't every day I come home to find a hot frat bro in my bed."

"You think I'm hot?"

He eyes my exposed body, my toned stomach, which I'm actually kind of proud of, and the tight muscles on my chest. "Hell, yeah." He moves closer to me and I gasp. "I couldn't help notice you were saying my name."

"Yeah, I guess I was fantasizing..."

"Are you interested in making that fantasy come true?"

I smile nervously. "I... I've never done this before."

"You mean sex, or sex with a man?"

"Both," I answer shyly.

Edward's eyes brighten. "So you're a virgin?"

I nod. "But I'd like to change that."

Edward cups my face in his hand and our mouths crash together. His lips tickle mine, his dark beard scratching my soft skin. Then his tongue explores my mouth, cautious at first. I part my lips to let him in, and our tongues wrestle.

I surrender. He takes control of my mouth, places his hand on the small of my back and leads me to the bed. I settle in while he takes off his shorts.

Between kisses, I can't help taking a peek at the goods. His cock is every bit as magnificent as I imagined. Thick and long, with a smooth head that glistens like glass.

"Can I taste you?" I ask between kisses.

He leans back and smiles. "As much as you want."

He makes himself comfortable on the bed, pulls his shirt over his head and reveals his meaty biceps. His muscles flex as he joins his hands behind his head. He looks so confident, so carefree.

I take hold of him, the first time I've ever felt another man's cock in my hand. It's warm and soft and hard all at once. I feel him pulsing in my grip.

I lean forward and take him into my mouth, clumsy at first as I try to keep my lips pulled over my teeth. Though I know very little about giving a blowjob, I at least know enough not to scrape.

He tastes clean against my tongue, like soap and something else, something new. The taste of a man. I relish in the flavor, swallowing as much as I can, but I only make it partway down his shaft before I start to gag and choke.

"Go slow," he says softly, running his fingers through my hair.

I relax and pull back, then try again, this time taking him a little deeper. He groans in response, throws his head back as I swirl my tongue up to his cock head.

"That's good, Lance," he says with a satisfied sigh.

I like the raspy way he says my name.

While I explore his cock with my mouth, my fingers explore his abs, which flex and tighten as I run my hands along the cascading ridges.

My fingertips find their way to his nipples. I pinch one and twist it lightly. He gasps.

"Wait," he says breathlessly. "You're getting me close."

I pull off and smile up at him. "Is that a bad thing?"

"No," he says, grinning, "but I'm not ready yet. I want to taste you."

"Oh." I feel myself blushing. I lean back and present myself on his bed.

Edward takes charge again, pulling my legs apart and diving between my thighs. His tongue is like magic, his mouth all over me. He sucks and slurps my dripping cock with ease. I shudder as he swallows me whole. He bobs his head up and down a few times, then he's down at my balls, twirling his wicked tongue around them.

And before I can catch my breath, he's moved to my thighs, kissing and biting at them. He's turning me into a squirming, moaning mess.

He delves deeper once more, licking a stripe underneath my balls. I gasp in surprise, tingling all over. Fuck, I never knew I was so sensitive there. And then he spreads my ass cheeks apart. The lower half of his face disappears, his nose resting on my nut sack, and I feel a new and exciting sensation as he digs and twists his tongue inside my hole like a corkscrew.

"Oh, god," I moan, "that feels so good."

"I'm just getting started," Edward murmurs.

He soaks his middle finger in spit, licking up the sides of his digit like a popsicle, then slowly I feel him pressing the pad of his fingertip into my hole. I shudder as he works his way inside, sliding all the way to his knuckle. Then I feel his finger bend inward and he lands on that spot inside me that feels like heaven.

My whole body quakes as he masterfully strums me like a guitar. I make music with my sighs, my gasps and breathy groans.

All the while, my cock feels impossibly hard, crying a river of desperate precum all over my stomach.

Edward proceeds to eat me while he fingers my hole, sending ribbons of pleasure both inside and out of me.

"Please fuck me," I beg, my body shaking. "I want you so bad."

Edward grins. "You do, huh?"

I bite my lip and nod. "Yes, please. I can't wait anymore." I grab the bottle of lube and hand it to him.

"Bossy little virgin, aren't you?" he says. His eyes twinkle and a dimple forms in his cheek. He retrieves a condom from his drawer and offers it to me. "I'll let you do the honors."

I tear along the edge of the packet, pull out the rubber ring and place it on top of his cock like a crown. Then I slide it down, feeling the way it clings to his hot, hard shaft inch by inch until I've rolled it down to his low-hanging nuts.

He takes the lube and coats his cock in a thick layer. Then he spreads more of it along my trembling hole, working it inside me.

My eyes grow wide as I watch him aim his cock head against me. Fuck, this is real. It's happening. Two days ago, I would have never imagined letting a man take me this way. But now I'm horny and needy and I can't wait to feel my hot older neighbor inside me.

"You ready for me to take this ass?" he says playfully.

"Oh, god, yes. Take all of me."

"I'm taking it and making it mine." He presses slowly but firmly against me, and I feel myself break open around the impossible girth of him. He's so much thicker than the toy. I grit my teeth as he probes inside me.

"Just take a deep breath." His voice soothes me.

At first it burns as I feel the stretch. My body opening and awaking.

"Damn, you're tight." He sighs and his eyes flutter as he sinks inside me.

I feel my walls spreading open, squeezing and flexing to accommodate his girth. And soon the burn becomes an ache, the ache becomes a throb, and as he takes a few dips in and out of me, I feel my muscles relax. I surrender to the pleasure.

Edward thrusts himself to the hilt. His big balls slap against my ass. We moan in unison, his hands grabbing my hips, holding me in place as he pounds my tight, virgin hole.

Then he looks down at me, and his eyes are glazed as if he's lost in a blissful high.

"Is this what you wanted?" he asks.

"Yes." I claw at his shoulders, holding on to the thick, round edges.

"Sneaking into my house to jack off. Sneaking into my bed to fuck yourself with my toys."

"Yes," I moan.

"Imagining it was me. Imagining I was pounding your pink little hole."

"Oh, yeah..."

He starts pounding me faster, driving his hard cock all the way inside me. He steals my breath away when he hits that magical spot behind my balls.

Then he grabs my cock in his hand. It's soaked with precum. He uses my juices to create friction, fisting his palm up and down my shaft in rhythm as he fucks me.

My body is humming, vibrating inside and out.

"I'm close, Edward," I say, desperate with desire.

"So am I," he moans.

"Oh, god, oh, god." I'm helpless as he pounds the orgasm out of me, battering my insides while he strokes my slick cock. Then the fever breaks and I explode all over myself, ribbons of cum painting my skin.

The veins in Edward's neck bulge, his chest is flushed red as I feel his cock explode inside me. His body shakes as he empties his nuts, thrusting himself in and out until there's nothing left to give.

He flashes a satisfied grin and cuddles up beside me. It doesn't seem to matter to either of us that we're a sticky, sweaty mess. He lifts his arm and I catch a whiff of his raw masculinity as he pulls me against his heaving chest.

"I bet you're glad John bailed on the house sitting job," I say.

"Oh, definitely," Edward agrees. "His ass was nowhere near as tight as yours."

"Wait, what?" I blink at him in disbelief, then catch the smug way his lip curls. We both laugh. I tweak his nipple hard and he yelps.

"Have you had anything for breakfast?" he asks.

"Besides your man meat?" I smile. "No."

"Why don't we take a shower and then I'll make us some breakfast. I cook a great Western omelet."

"I'd love that."

As I follow my beefy neighbor toward the bathroom, I can't help but watch as his delectable ass moves with each step.

"So, I guess since you own a dildo, it's safe to assume you're versatile?" I ask.

He smiles over his shoulder. "Maybe after breakfast, you can find out."

With that, my cock is standing up like a flagpole. "I don't think I can wait," I say enthusiastically.

"Oh, to be nineteen again." Edward chuckles. "Grab the lube and another condom. I'll meet you in the shower."

It's only the second day of vacation, and I can't wait to see what sexy fun adventures this summer will bring...

BIG NICK ENERGY

CHAPTER 1

"See ya later, babe." I give a quick peck on the cheek before slinking out of the bedroom of my latest conquest.

She grabs my hand, looks up at me with sleepy eyes. "You'll text me later?" I know she just needs some reassurance before she drifts off to dreamland.

"Definitely." I squeeze her hand twice, smile at her all big and dopey, knowing my dimples are working their magic. Girls love my dimples.

And with that, I'm gone, like a thief in the night. The floral scent of her perfume still lingers on my skin.

I will not be texting her later.

And she will not be texting me, either.

The number I gave her is off by one digit. The name I gave her is fake, too. My name's Nick, but I said Rick. Oops. She must have misheard me over the loud music at the bar.

If I ever happen to bump into her, I'll pretend it was a mistake and offer her another phone number, which will also be incorrect. But I doubt we'll ever see each other again. I never hit the same bar twice. I take different rotations in different parts of the city. Sometimes I even go to the suburbs or other towns nearby.

That's what I love about living in California. There are so many beautiful women. All the time, everywhere you go. Sorority girls, tourists from out of town, best friends who are visiting for the summer or the holidays. Even the cougars catch my eye sometimes. My life feels like an endless buffet. And college is a never-ending party.

Twenty minutes later, I roll up to the frat house I call home. It's after midnight, but the lights are still on when I park along the curb.

I strut inside to find my bros hanging out. A few of them are piled onto the couch playing video games on the massive TV we all chipped in to buy.

"Whaaatup, Nick!?" my roommate, Jackson, says to me, all loud and enthusiastic like he always is. He peeps my wrinkled shirt and a few buttons I carelessly left undone. "Are you doing the Friday night walk of shame?"

"More like the Friday Night walk of *game*." I give him a fist bump as I shuffle past.

The boys in the next room erupt into laughter and start cheering. "Big Nick Energy! Big Nick Energy! Big Nick Energy!"

Ever since a few of the guys caught a glimpse of my big dick in the locker room, my nickname has been a running joke. You might see people on social media talk about 'Big Dick Energy' or #BDE to describe a guy who has the swagger or the confidence of being blessed with a big dick. So in my case, they turned Big Dick Energy into Big Nick Energy.

I make my way into the kitchen and bust into a proud smile. "What's up, guys?"

They're all grins and high-fives as they greet me. A few of them are sitting on bar stools around the kitchen island, and others are seated at the dining table playing cards. I swipe a slice of pepperoni pizza from an open box and bite off a chunk. Sexing ladies really works up my appetite.

"Dude, you owe me five dollars," Lucas says to Connor.

"Yeah, I know." Connor pulls out his phone and sends money through a cash app.

"You guys were taking bets on me?"

Lucas smirks. "Yeah, man. Connor didn't believe me when I told him you'd be going out again tonight. You just hooked up with a different girl last night."

"Was it just last night?" I scratch the scruff on my chin. "I thought it was two nights ago."

"No, two nights ago was when we went out drinking and you plowed the bartender in the bathroom," Lucas offers.

My memory is so hazy, I can't even remember her face. All I recall is meeting someone in a stall and drunkenly taking her from behind. I vaguely remember the back of her head. I think she had black hair, or maybe brown. "Damn, guys, I didn't realize I'd been so busy this week."

Connor snorts. "You do this every week. It's why you've got that Big Nick Energy."

I grab my crotch and give it a firm shake. "What can I say? This big boy likes to have a good time. And the ladies love it." My bros start laughing and break out into another round of chants.

I come by my nickname honestly. With a twelve-inch dick, I'm the envy of all my buds. I'm just blessed with what God gave me, and I love to share.

"So who did you hook up with tonight?" Connor asks.

I shrug. "I think her name was Brittany. Or Tiffany. Wait, no, something with an 'M.' Shit, I dunno. She was some sexy little blonde I met at a place by the boardwalk."

"Was she able to take the whole thing?" Lucas asks.

"Wouldn't you like to know, you horny homo." I play-punch him in the arm. "Nah, but she gave it her best shot. I think she was able to fit about three or four inches in her mouth before she started gagging and drooling all over my nuts. I didn't get to bone her, though. She said she was afraid I'd stretch her out so she gave me a hand job instead.

"Sorry, bro," Lucas says.

"It's alright. Comes with the territory."

It's sad, but true. Having a big dick is fun to show off, and I love the attention. But most girls have trouble getting past my fat mushroom head. I've never met someone who can take everything I've got. If I ever do, I swear I'm gonna ask her to marry me on the spot.

"What's the longest you've ever gone without hooking up?" Connor asks.

"Hell, I don't know." I try to remember my first two years of college, and then my senior year of high school. "A week, maybe, when I was younger. It wasn't as easy in high school. Word got around."

"A week?" Lucas snorts and shakes his head. "It's been *months* since I had a date."

"Ya gotta put yourself out there," I say.

Lucas loud-whispers to Connor. "I bet he couldn't last two weeks without hooking up with a girl."

I puff up my chest. "Bullshit."

"No way." Lucas turns toward me. "Two weeks would destroy you."

"Hey, you guys are acting like I have no self-control. I bet I could even go three weeks if I really wanted."

Wait, shut up, Nick. I don't know why I'm trying to make a bet I can't win. But something competitive is stirring inside me. Looking at the way they all smirk, so certain they have me figured out. They even take bets on my social habits. I feel like a tool.

"Make it a full month and we'll have a deal," Lucas says. I can tell by the way his eyes gleam that he's certain I will say no. *Big Nick is too weak*, he's probably thinking.

"A full month, huh?" My nuts ache just imagining going that long. "What are the stakes?"

"I'll put fifty dollars down that says you'll never make it. If you do—which you definitely won't—the money is yours."

"Are you serious?" Connor asks. Lucas nods. "Okay, then, I'll put twenty on that."

"Hold up, let me write this down." Lucas starts tapping away at his phone screen. "Okay, fifty for me. Twenty for Connor."

Jon and Clay chime in. They each want to put up fifty of their own. The guys from the living room want in on the action, too, so they add in a couple hundred. Lucas calls upstairs to the guys in their rooms and asks if they want to add to the pot.

My head is spinning wondering what I've gotten myself into. A whole month without sex sounds insane. But some extra cash sure would be nice.

Five of my brothers clomp down the stairs and funnel into the kitchen. Leading the gang is Andre, who's the top dog of the house. He's a good guy, deep down, but he's bossy as hell and always wants to control everyone. When he hears about the bet, he leers in a way that makes my stomach clench.

"How much are we up to?" Andre asks after everyone has committed to a share.

"Seven-twenty-five," Lucas says.

I can't believe my ears. "Seven-hundred-twenty-five dollars? And all I have to do is not fuck a girl for a month?"

"Let's raise the stakes, boys," Andre says. "I'll bring us up to an even thousand."

"A thousand?" Lucas asks.

Andre nods confidently. "But there's a catch."

"Of course," I mutter.

"Hey, a thousand dollars is a lot." His brown eyes twinkle with mischief. "I think it's only fair that we get some extra insurance."

"Okay." I feel sweat beading on my forehead.

"We're gonna lock your dick in a cage." Andre flashes all his teeth. "Keep that Big Nick Energy nice and snug for a whole month."

"A cage? What the hell are you talking about?"

Andre whips out his phone and pounds in a search with his fat fingertips. When he finds what he's looking for, he smiles and holds the phone out to me. I stare at the foreign device, not sure what I'm looking at.

"It's called a chastity cage," Andre explains. "Your dick stays in that steel tube. And it connects to a cock ring that goes around your nuts and the base of your shaft. Everything is held in place. I'll put a mini padlock on to make sure you don't cheat."

My mouth hangs open. I can't quite comprehend the concept. "I'd wear this all the time?"

Andre nods. "Yep. It's rust-proof and skin safe. You can piss through it, take a shower in it, whatever. The only thing you can't do is your favorite thing. You'll wear it for the entire month."

"What about boners?"

With a laugh, Andre says, "Big Nick is no match for steel. Your dick will learn."

"Andre, come on. This is crazy. Can't you just trust me?" I look around the room. All eyes are on me, and every single face is filled with doubt. Nobody thinks I can do it.

"We're talking about a thousand dollars. Easy money. You just have to wear this for a month."

I look to Connor, searching for some guidance. He always knows what to do. "It's your choice," he says quietly.

"If I lose, do I have to pay you guys?"

Andre shakes his head. "Of course not, Nick. We're all brothers here. Nobody expects you to cough up that much money on your own. It's really simple. Winner takes all, or else nobody pays a cent. It's the easiest cash you'll ever make."

"Easy money, huh?" I can't imagine going that long without sex. Usually I have to bust a nut at least once a day. Sometimes twice if I'm really amped up. A month will be impossible. But I know my brothers have my back. If I lose, it'll be alright. No harm, no foul. "Okay. I'm in."

"Good." Andre shakes my hand. His grip is strong, powerful. "I know a place that's open all night. They'll have just what we're looking for. Let's go."

At this very moment, I know my fate is sealed. The guys are all counting on me to fail. I refuse to lose this bet.

CHAPTER 2

The street is dead. Not a soul in sight, and the only sound is the unsettling whisper of the wind. But one small window burns bright amidst the shadows. A neon pink sign hangs over the door: *Open 24 hours.*

"What is this place?" I ask.

Andre eyes me like I'm asking the stupidest question he's ever heard. "An adult novelty store. You've never been?"

I shake my head, annoyed at the way he's acting. "No, I haven't. The first clue might have been when I asked what this place was."

"Alright, alright, no need for that." He slings his arm around my shoulder like we're best buds. "They sell sex toys here."

"Well that explains it then. You don't need sex toys when you've got this." I gesture to my crotch.

Andre pats my chest a little too hard. "Not for long, you don't."

We step inside. I'm surprised to find the store is clean and well-lit. Mannequins are prominently displayed, their ghost-white bodies modeling lacy red lingerie on the female and some sort of shiny black briefs on the male.

There's a tiered table in the center where all sorts of colorful toys are displayed next to bottles of lubricant. This is not what I expected. Many of the vibrators are bright, playful hues of pink and purple. There are a few traditional penis-style toys mixed in, with flesh-colored skin and detailed veins.

"Dude, why are we in a dildo store?" I ask.

"Relax. The cages are in the back." Andre tilts his head toward the rear of the store.

"And why do you know this information?"

He grins as he struts down the aisle. "You're not the first guy to lose a bet in our house."

"I haven't lost anything. That thousand dollars is mine."

"We'll see."

We breeze past rows of odd and interesting playthings. Handcuffs and ball gags. Silky nighties and leather chaps. My pulse races as I imagine the scenarios. I could have a lot of fun in a place like this.

Andre stops in front of a glass display case. A burly dude is behind the counter. Colorful tattoos wind around his arms, disappear underneath his shirt, and continue along his neck.

"Can I help you guys?" the man asks.

Andre points through the case to what looks like a medieval torture device. "Yeah, we need one of those in a size small."

"Size small?! There's no way I'm gonna fit in a small."

"You'll fit," Andre and the man say in unison. Their eyes meet and they share knowing smiles. This feels like a game that everyone knows the rules to except for me.

"Do you need a fitting room?" the man asks.

"Yeah, that would be great," Andre says.

"A fitting room?" I whisper. "Bro, I don't need your help getting that on. I can take care of it myself."

"What are the stakes?" the employee asks.

"Big Nick here is putting his big dick into lock-up for a month," Andre explains. "If he makes it, he gets a thousand dollars. But he won't make it."

The employee shoots me a smarmy grin, licks his teeth, then shakes his head. "Nope."

"You're both wrong," I huff. "Give me the cage. I'm winning this bet."

The employee hands the chastity device to Andre instead of me. I notice the man won't address me directly, like I'm not even a person. Does he think Andre is my handler or something?

We head over to a changing room. Andre steps inside with me. The small space is brightly lit with mirrors at every angle.

"Drop your drawers," Andre instructs.

I undo my jeans and let them fall to my ankles. Andre's eyes grow wide as he takes in the sight of my meaty manhood. "Are you completely soft?"

I put my hands on my hips and stand proudly in a Superman pose. "Yep, seven inches soft, twelve inches hard.

I've got a true foot-long down there. So how do you expect me to fit in a small?"

Andre smiles deviously. "You'll fit." He takes apart the device and sets the spare pieces on a beat-up and stained chair. The first piece is a gleaming steel ring, which he pushes my cock into and then squeezes my nut sack through the hoop.

"Fuck, that's cold." I try to pull away but Andre holds me captive by my balls. Then, things go from awkward to just plain humiliating as I feel the blood rush to my shaft.

"Don't get hard."

"I'm not trying to, but when someone holds my dick, I tend to react."

He slaps my nuts. The pain comes fast and hot, burning bright with a simultaneous urge to puke. "Fucking hell," I squeak.

Andre reaches between my legs and pokes my cock inside me like an accordion. I didn't know that was possible. Then he stuffs what's left of my limp dick into the impossibly small metal tube and threads the clips together with the ring. Everything snaps into place while I'm still blind with pain. The final nail in the proverbial coffin is when he snaps the lock shut. I hear it echo in my ears.

When I've finally recovered enough to see straight and stand upright, I'm stunned to find myself stuffed tight in the cage. My flared cock head strains against the metal bars of the headpiece. I can't even see the rest of my dick. It's all mashed together inside me.

"How's it feel?" Andre asks.

"You tell me." I swing for his nuts but he dodges my punch, sending me hurling toward the other wall. We both bust out laughing. "Quick reflexes you've got there."

He nods. "Bro, I gotta confess, I can't believe you're really going for this."

"Neither can I." I examine my reflection from every angle of the surrounding mirrors. Gone is the big one-eyed beast that has always hung between my legs. All that's left of me is a tiny nub trapped in steel and two very plump balls which now seem oddly bigger than my cock. "How do I go to the bathroom?"

Andre handles my imprisoned manhood and points it upward so I can get a good view. The tip of the cage has an open circle that's just large enough for fluids to pass. "Your piss hole lines up with the center. You see that? You'll have a clear shot. But you might want to sit down to avoid any messy splashing."

His warm hand is strangely soothing, and I feel myself straining against my confined cage. "What happens if I get hard?"

"Like I said earlier, you're no match for steel. If you *try* to get hard, your nuts will get crunched between the shaft piece and the ring."

"And if I need to unlock?"

"Then you come to me." He dangles a double set of keys in front of my face. "Don't worry, Nick. I'll take care of you."

CHAPTER 3

If it weren't for pure exhaustion, I don't think I would have slept at all last night. The constant tugging on my locked manhood was driving me out of my mind. My underwear was a mess, a puddle of pre-cum dripping slowly from the tap. Thankfully I was so tired that I fell asleep as soon as my head hit the pillow.

Today was a challenge but I kept myself busy. This morning I went to the park with a few of my buds. We kicked around the soccer ball a bit, just hung out and enjoyed the nice weather. It was kind of overcast and breezy.

Word had gotten around about my chastity device, and everyone thought it was a joke. I assured them it wasn't. I wanted them to know I was serious about that cash, so they'd better be ready to cough it up. A couple of guys even wanted to see the cage. I told them I wasn't down for a show. Not yet anyway.

I'm still pretty self-conscious about how tiny my dick looks. I'm used to being Big Nick, not little dick.

We played video games in the afternoon, then a group of us cooked dinner together and finished off the evening watching TV. Our house is always alive with good conversation and laughter. That's what I love about being in a fraternity. It's a bond, a brotherhood.

The guys kept asking to see my dick. All it did was remind me of how horny and frustrated I felt. I had to change my underwear two times just to avoid creating a wet spot on my pants from all the leakage.

Things finally quieted down around midnight, and I headed into the library at the back of the house. It's the only space where we have a rule for everyone to keep the volume down. No laughing, no hanging out just to make noise. I usually go there to study. But now I just need to clear my head.

I walk over to one of the massive windows, which has floor-to-ceiling glass and an awesome view of the park behind our house.

"Long day?" a voice asks from the shadows.

My heart jumps. I look to the corner to find Andre sitting in an oversized armchair. "Damn, man. I didn't know anyone was in here."

He leans forward, his face now visible in the moonlight. "Sorry."

"It was a good day," I say. "I'm just trying to stay busy."

"To keep your mind off the bet?"

"Not that anyone will let me forget about it." I walk over to Andre's side.

"You can always cave if you want. I could unlock you right now and send you on your way to the bars. I bet it would feel so good to unload in some hottie."

My stomach flutters just thinking about how good it would be. I feel another strand of fluid pulse out of me. But I resist the temptation. "Not a chance, man."

Andre shrugs. "It's your choice. Always your choice. Are you having any trouble with chaffing or pinching?"

"No. Just dealing with a river down there. I've never seen so much pre-cum. It's like my balls are ready to bust."

"Your prostate."

"Huh?"

"It's not your balls, it's your prostate gland." Andre stands and fills the space between us. He's taller than I am by a few inches, and I'm 6-foot-1. "Your prostate is swollen."

"Makes sense, I guess. I usually blow my wad at least once a day."

"Do I need to get you some maxi-pads?" Andre shoots me a toothy grin.

"No, asshole." I jokingly push his arm, but he doesn't budge. He's all muscle.

"If you're really feeling the pressure, there's a way to get some relief."

I raise an eyebrow. "Oh, yeah?"

"I could give you a prostate massage."

"Okay, whatever, Andre." Now I know he's messing with me. "I think I'm gonna head to bed, try and get some sleep."

"Suit yourself." He pats me on the shoulder and walks ahead of me. I catch a whiff of his spicy cologne, and it hits me in a weird way. Damn, I really must be desperate if sniffing guys turns me on.

Unfortunately, my efforts to sleep are hopeless. I toss and turn under the covers for almost an hour, trying to get comfortable. I'm hot and sweaty, although the room is its usual crisp 68 degrees.

"Everything okay over there?" Jackson asks. His bed is against the left wall, and mine is against the right side. A large desk with two chairs sits in front of the window between us.

"Yeah, man, sorry. Am I keeping you awake?"

He rustles around and rolls over to face the wall. "It's fine," he murmurs.

I pull out my phone and check the time. It's 1:11. I wonder if Andre is still awake.

I tap out a quick message: *Are you up?*

Within seconds, Andre responds: *Yes. Having trouble sleeping?*

Yes.

My offer stands.

Can you keep a secret?

Of course. Meet me in the backyard.

CHAPTER 4

There's a chill in the air as I make my way behind the soaring evergreen trees. A bunch of overgrown shrubs border the back of our property along the fence line, offering an extra privacy barrier against the park.

"Andre, are you out here?" I whisper.

"Right here," he says into my ear. His breath is warm against my neck. My skin breaks out into goosebumps.

"Jesus, man, could you be any more creepy?"

He steps in front of me. "Sorry. I was just answering your question."

"Whatever," I huff. "So how will this work?"

"I have a latex glove and a tube of lubricant here in my pocket. What I'll do is slowly enter your rectum with a well-lubricated, gloved finger. Then I'll gently stimulate your prostate gland until I've milked out some of that pent-up fluid."

"You sound like a med student. How do you know this stuff?"

His teeth shine in the moonlight. "I have my secrets."

"Hooking up and getting fingered behind some trees sounds pretty gay."

"Are you attracted to men?"

I shake my head. "Of course not."

"Then it's not gay."

My dick has a mind of its own. All this talk about releasing fluids has caused me to leak with even more pre-cum. "You really think this will help?"

"It's basic anatomy, bro."

I'm aching so badly with blocked pipes, I figure I'll do anything to get some relief. "And if I do this, the bet is still on?"

"We agreed you'd stay locked and wouldn't hook up with any girls for a month, right?"

"Right."

"Then you aren't breaking any rules." Andre's voice is low and husky. It's turning my stomach inside out.

"Okay, let's give it a try."

"We can stop any time you want." I hear him pull the glove over his hand. It snaps against his wrist, and I feel myself coming undone with anticipation. My eyes have adjusted to the darkness, and I can see him squeezing out a generous ribbon of lube onto his fingertip. Then he rubs his digits together, warming them up. "You might want to take your pants off for this."

I follow his instructions and set my jeans on a nearby patio chair. I feel so vulnerable standing outside half-naked, with my big dick reduced to a tiny little button.

"Just relax," he says, placing a warm hand on my shoulder. With his gloved hand, he gently strokes a line between my ass cheeks. "Widen your stance, please."

He tickles the knot of my butthole. It's a strange, tingling sensation I've never experienced. I let out a jagged breath, a bundle of nerves inside as another fat glob of fluid leaks freely from my dick head.

With a firm but careful amount of pressure, he begins stroking my hole, dipping his finger ever so slightly inside. At first, my body resists, my hole clenching tight. But with each soft stroke, I feel him sinking just a little more inside, and soon I begin to relax.

"You'll feel some slight pushback," he says. "It's your muscles contracting. But once I make my way past the barrier, your body will open up for me."

"Okay." I nod and take a big breath.

It happens exactly as he described. First, it feels impossible. I've tightened up and there's no way he's breaking through. But then it's like a cave crumbles, and his finger glides effortlessly inside. I let out a sigh of relief. There's a slight twinge of discomfort, but it doesn't hurt like I thought it would.

"Are you okay?" Andre's deep voice is soothing music to my ears.

"Mmm-hmm," I breathe out.

Everything inside me tingles. I'm not sure if I love it, if I hate it, but I feel ticklish all over. And then his fingertip brushes against something inside me that makes me fall apart.

"Oh, fuck," I say with a shudder.

"That's the magic spot," he says into my ear. It's then that I realize how close he's standing to my backside. We're not touching, but I can feel the heat of his presence towering over me. "Just keep breathing deep and let yourself let go."

His finger traces circles around inside me, gentle but probing. It reminds me of summertime in the pool, when I swim around in a circle, building a whirlpool. That's what's happening now, and the current builds somewhere deep and private, a place I've never explored.

I've lost all control. Pre-cum is flowing from my trapped cock in long, thick ropes. And the waves keep building. I haven't hit the crest yet, I just keep feeling better and better.

"Fuck, Andre, I don't know what you're doing to me."

"It's all you, bud," he whispers. "Your body's doing the work. You just needed someone to flip the switch."

He's wrong. I'm breathless and needy. I couldn't do this without him. He's unlocked something inside me that feels better than anything I've experienced with my dick. Unlocked, yet locked, all at once.

"I feel... Damn, I feel... I don't know what's coming over me..." My voice goes high and kind of whiny, but I don't care. I'm way past shyness as I grind my bottom against Andre's masterful hand. I just want him to keep touching me this way forever.

"Let go, Nick." His lips are so close, I'd swear they're about to brush my earlobe. "Let go, and you'll be free."

I fall back against him. My legs are shaky and unsteady. I can hardly keep my balance. But Andre is there for me with his strong hand, twirling circles inside my wet hole. His free hand grips my bicep and squeezes. "Fuck, Andre," I moan. "Fuck."

Everything feels hazy, like a dream, and I never want to wake up. And then I'm met with a new surprise as Andre squeezes a second finger inside me. His thick digits fill me. I'm stuffed full to the brim. Hell, it might as well be a dick inside me, I feel packed so tight. But it's good. So damn good as he changes his technique and starts applying more concentrated pressure directly on my sweet spot.

I feel as if my body is vibrating. My nipples harden, my whole core tenses with anticipation. The waves keep building, building, higher and higher. My dick strains against the relentless metal bars that hold it captive, but nothing can hold back this hurricane.

"Oh, god. Andre, Andre, I think..." My words are cut short by the explosion from my locked cock. Thick splatters of white hot release, one after the other, shooting out of my useless nub. I reach down and try to stroke it, but all I can do is squeeze my nuts tight in my hand as Andre works the last drops out of me.

I collapse into his arms, breathing heavily while my head is light.

"How do you feel?" Andre asks, wrapping his arms around me. I don't even mind. In fact I snuggle in tighter, letting him possess me.

"Like a thousand bucks."

CHAPTER 5

I wake up from the best night's sleep I've ever had. Truly I don't know if I've ever felt so good. But frustration sets in as soon as I feel the needy ache between my legs.

When I pull back the covers, I find my weak effort at morning wood straining against my cage. My nuts are pulled tight against the ring that binds them, and the head of my cock burns bright red as it smashes itself against the bars of its prison cell. If only I could hold onto the euphoria from last night a little longer.

I close my eyes and replay a memory that now feels so far away. The light of the moon. The pinewood in the wind. The heat of Andre's body pressed against mine, and the skillful way he twirled his magic fingertips, summoning an explosion from inside me that I didn't know was possible without touching my cock.

But my thoughts only cause me to start dripping again, the insistent leaking of my useless nob. I don't know how I'm going to make it the rest of the month without letting the guys call my bluff. Everyone's counting on me to give up. I can't. I won't.

As I get out of bed and pull on some shorts, I start to laugh when I think about it. I was so desperate for relief that I had a guy finger me until I shot my load.

And strangely, I kind of want it to happen again.

My thoughts return to Andre. The gleam in his eyes. The crooked way his mouth spreads into a smile.

No, this is gay. *What's the matter with me?*

I should be thinking about the soft, pink spread of a woman's...dick.

Wait, what?

My mind has wandered back to Andre, curious about his cock. I wonder if it's as large and as hard as his muscles. I wonder if it would stuff me tight the way his fingers do. Stretch my virgin hole out until...

I shake away all these confusing thoughts. I've really gotta get my mind on something else. I head to the hallway toward the bathroom. The door's locked and I can hear someone turning off the shower head, then the sound of the curtain rings sliding on the track. I figure whoever's in there will be out in a minute, so I lean against the doorframe.

Moments later, the door opens. Andre floats out from a cloud of steam. His chest glistens with beads of water, his torso a perfectly sculpted specimen, tight and lean with abs that pop with each defined muscle.

"Good morning, Nick," he says too cheerfully. I don't remember him ever being this friendly to me. Has he changed, or have I?

My eyes dart down to his hips, to the canvas of honey-brown skin that disappears underneath his towel. As if reading my mind, he taunts me. His wicked fingertips pull the towel open just enough to flash a glimpse of lush dark pubic hair. And then he closes the gap once more, tightens the towel, tucks it securely along his waist. My cock rebels against its cage, a drooling dog tethered to its leash. It can growl all it wants but it can't break free.

"Uh, morning," I mumble, swallowing the excess saliva that's pooled on my tongue.

I can't meet his gaze. I don't dare. If I look into his eyes, I fear I'll come completely undone. So instead, I edge past him, brushing against his warm arm as I slink into the bathroom.

The space is filled with the scent of his body wash. Warm and woodsy, kind of like a lumberjack bathed in sweet juniper berries.

"Good talk," he says as I close the door in his face.

But then I spy something on the floor that threatens to destroy my sanity. A balled-up garment lays in the corner against the tub.

God, no, please. Please don't let that be his underwear.

I pick up the grey boxer-briefs with my fingertips, holding them far away like they're a bomb. The silky athletic material feels so nice against my skin.

I shouldn't...

I couldn't...

But I want to...

Slowly, ever so carefully, I bring Andre's underwear close to my face. The fabric is still warm, filled with the heat of his body, his nuts that were cradled all nice and snug in the pouch. I want to bury my face inside. I want to stick out my tongue and taste...

A tap at the door stops me.

"Hey, Nick, I think I left my drawers in there."

Disappointment floods my veins. I quickly open the door and toss Andre his underwear. Now I'm free from the temptation.

Damn it, I was just about to bury my face in a dude's dirty underwear. What is coming over me?

I need an ice-cold shower to soothe this restless desire.

CHAPTER 6

I made it through the day without busting a nut or sniffing anyone's underwear. A miracle, I know.

After breakfast, I studied for an exam. Then I hung out with some of the guys. Thankfully Andre was nowhere around. That was a small gift to my sanity.

I've made it to the evening, and now the guys are planning on having some friends over for beer and fun. We gather in the basement, which has been converted into a rec room. Guests start funneling in around eight. There's a ping pong table which nobody uses for its intended purpose. I wouldn't know where to find the paddles if I needed them. Instead, the table is lined with red Solo cups, standing in formation for the inevitable game of beer pong.

There are some hot-looking girls from the nearby sorority. I recognize a few that I've seen around. They wave at me and I give a coy wave back. I try to act shy. It's part of my charm. Then I flash a dimpled smile and pretend to blush.

The ladies look hot as hell, with low-cut tops and tight little shorts, which leave little to the imagination. Big Nick would be all over them in an instant. But all I can think about is Andre. I scan the room, wondering if he'll be coming down soon.

I stop by the pool table, where Clay and Jon are playing a game. "Hey, have you guys seen Andre?"

Jon shakes his head. "Haven't seen him all day," Clay says.

Damn. I feel my heart sink. I wonder where Andre could be.

I try to make the most of the night, try to swallow down my desperation. I feel like some sort of needy chick, hanging around, waiting for a guy who may not show. A pang of guilt strikes as I wonder if that's how women feel when they never see me again. Do they go back to the place we met, hoping to run into me?

By ten, I realize I've done nothing but watch the clock for two hours. I sit on the couch in a huff. Everyone around me is happy and buzzing with energy. And all I can think about is *him*.

"Hey, who's up for some strip poker?" Some girl is holding a bottle of vodka. She whips her blonde hair over her shoulders and eyes the room. Our guests cheer and a bunch of them settle onto the couch where I'm sitting alone, enjoying my pity party. "Do you mind if I sit here?" the girl asks after she's already seated herself and is halfway on my lap.

"Sure," I say glumly, not even feeling a spark as her bare legs brush against mine.

The guys deal out the cards on the coffee table in front of me. I decide to play along, not thinking far enough ahead to realize this is a truly terrible idea.

I'm halfway committed to the game while keeping my eyes on the staircase, hoping Andre will suddenly appear. The game unfolds around me, a bustle of background noise that I barely comprehend. I finally snap back to reality when the girl beside me nudges my arm.

"How many cards do you want?" she asks.

"Huh?" I say distractedly. "Oh, three."

I lose the first game, not that I really care, so I remove my shirt and drop it in my lap.

Andre is still nowhere to be found. I think about texting him, but that would sound clingy. I don't want him to know the effect he has on me.

Soon, everyone around me is nearly naked. I think they're purposely losing the game, judging by their loud drunken laughter and the way they so enthusiastically start flinging shirts and shorts all over the place. I also think they're taking off more than one piece of closing with each turn.

I lose the second game, this time not even noticing that I'm holding my cards downward for everyone to see.

"Nick, you're definitely losing with that hand, buddy. You need to take something else off." It's Jackson who's speaking to me. He has to snap his fingers to get my attention.

I absent-mindedly slide down my shorts, not even caring where I set them.

"Oh, you're Nick?" the girl beside me asks. I meet her pretty hazel eyes for the first time.

"Yeah," I say.

Her face spreads into a grin. "Big Nick," she says. Now she's cuddling up close to me, her breasts pressed against my arm.

My brothers begin cheering. "Big Nick Energy! Big Nick Energy!" The whole room joins in. I feel my cheeks turning red, and this time, I'm not faking my shyness for attention.

"He's not Big Nick anymore," I hear a voice call out. I look over to see it's Lucas, smiling from ear to ear. He seems quite proud of himself for making the announcement.

"Dude," Connor says. "Not cool."

I look around. All eyes are on me. My heart starts pounding against my chest. I lick my lips, dry as the desert. "Nah, it's fine." I try to shrug it off. "It's true. The guys bet a thousand bucks I couldn't go the month without having sex. So I took the bet. They're wrong about me."

"Don't leave out the best part," Lucas says. "Nick's dick is locked up." He pauses for dramatic effect. "In a cage."

I shoot daggers at him with my eyes. So much for discretion.

"Wait, no way." The girl beside me grabs a handful of my junk, then recoils. "Ohmygod, it's all hard and weird. What is going on under there?"

I sigh, knowing this isn't a subject that's going away on its own. "I'm wearing a chastity cage. Basically it locks up my dick so I can't get hard."

"Ohmygod," the girl says again.

"Whatever. Can we get back to the game, please?" I say.

"It's your go, Nick," Lucas reminds me, all too eagerly. "What have you got in your hand?"

I look down to see a pair of threes. Instantly, I feel the heat creeping up my neck. It's too late to bluff my way out of this. I toss the cards down on the table.

"Only one more piece of clothing to take off," Lucas so helpfully reminds me.

Everyone is staring at the outline in my briefs. They're all expecting me to be ashamed, too. Run away like some little bitch. But that's not Nick. Not now, not ever. I never back down from a challenge.

I tilt my chin defiantly. "So you guys all wanna see what's under here?"

The crowd responds with wild enthusiasm. I take a deep breath, stand, and face the room.

"You know I'm still Big Nick," I say, hooking my thumbs into my waistband. "A month from now, I'll be letting this beast out of its cage and Big Nick Energy will be taking over the campus."

"Just show us your dick," a stranger says. I don't even know who he is and he comes into my house ordering me around.

But I try to play it cool. "Take it down a notch, homo. I know you're thirsty for this big D."

"Quit stalling," a husky voice commands from across the room. I look over to see it's Andre. He's leaning against the wall, arms folded across his chest, biceps bulging.

I swallow my pride and pull down my underwear. My eyes remain locked on Andre.

Then I hear a giggle. "I think he's trying to get hard," the girl beside me says. I look down to see her face is at eye level with my junk.

And she's right. My dick, with a stubborn mind of its own, is straining against the cage. A long rope of pre-cum oozes from the tip. Everyone sees it.

Another girl chimes in. "Ew, it's so pathetic."

"You couldn't pay me a million dollars to lock up my shit like that," some loudmouth guy adds, like anyone asked for his opinion.

Everyone is laughing. One of them is actually wiping away tears. I can't believe they think it's so funny seeing me like this. Humiliation swallows me up as I try to hide my needy cock with my hand. I cup myself and hurry out of the basement, leaving all my clothes behind.

This is all because of Andre.

CHAPTER 7

I bury myself in blankets, alone and embarrassed in my bed. There's a gentle knock outside my door. I already know who it is.

"What?" I bark.

"Can I come in?"

I peek my head up from under the covers. "Yeah, come on in."

The door slowly opens. Andre stands there, quiet and humble, yet his presence is commanding. I sit upright but keep myself covered. He closes the door behind him and pads across the room to my bedside. "May I sit?"

"Sure."

He takes a deep breath and lets it out. I feel it all over my arms, the heat that radiates from him. Our eyes are locked, but I don't sense any harm on his part. I imagine he's come in here to tell me what to do. He always likes to have the upper hand.

"There's no shame in quitting," he says softly. There it is. The advice I didn't ask for. I knew he just came in here to boss me around.

"And let you off the hook for the money?" I scoff. "I've already been humiliated in front of everyone. I can't back down now. They need to see me win."

"Nick," he says firmly, his Dad tone coming out in full effect. "Is this just about money? Because I sense there's something else."

"What do you mean?"

He sidesteps my question. "I had fun last night."

"Yeah, thanks for that." I try to keep a straight face, terrified I'll give something away.

"I have some massage oil back in my room. I could help ease some of this...tension."

"What if Clay comes up and finds us?"

"He was busy playing beer pong when I left. Besides, I can lock the door."

I eye Andre warily, look down at his large hands resting on his lap. His long, fat fingers. I think about the magic they weave. "Okay, I'll meet you in there. I need to grab some clothes."

"But you'll just be taking them off," Andre says.

"I'm not walking through the halls naked."

"Of course." Andre rises from my bed, and it's then that I see the massive bulge in his pants. Is he as excited about me as I am for him? He walks away with a slight squirm in his walk, like he's trying to adjust himself without using his hands.

I slide on a jockstrap to help contain the relentless leaking from my locked manhood, then throw on a pair of shorts and a shirt. Down the hall, Andre is waiting in his room. A candle is burning, filling the room with the sweet smell of vanilla. When I walk in, his gaze meets mine. The flicker of the candlelight dances like stars in his eyes.

"Go ahead and lock the door behind you." He unfolds a towel and spreads it across his bed.

I do as I'm told. My stomach feels full of butterflies as I watch the thoughtful way he's setting the scene.

He pops open a dark purple bottle of oil and begins rubbing it between his hands. "Make yourself comfortable," he says. I strip down to my jockstrap. He smiles approvingly. "Nice."

"How do you want me?" I ask. My cheeks grow warm as soon as the words spill past my lips.

"Lie flat, face down."

I slide onto his bed. His mattress is so soft. It's like sinking into a cloud. "Nice bed you have."

"Thanks," he says, slowly spreading his palms across my shoulders. "It's memory foam."

His touch feels like fire on my skin. I close my eyes and let out an involuntary moan.

"That's it, Nick. Let yourself melt into the feeling."

He applies gentle pressure to my shoulders, rubs his hands across my neck, then glides down my back in slow sweeps. His hands run all the way down my body, stopping just before he reaches the band of my jockstrap. Then he moves up again and rubs circles with his palms.

"You're not what I expected, Andre," I say.

"How's that?"

"You're always kind of bossing people around," I confess.

"I like to be in charge. Is that so wrong?"

I turn my head to see he's standing close to my face, and the protrusion in his pants is quite evident. "I guess not," I whisper hoarsely.

He chuckles. "You're a lot different than I expected, too. Always the party boy, always on the go."

"I don't like to stick around too long."

"Why do you think that is?" he asks.

"Because I have places to be."

"Big Nick Energy is hard to contain," he offers.

I nod my head against his impossibly soft bed. "Exactly."

"And yet, I have you contained and under my control." A smile pulls on his lips as I look up at him. "Don't worry, Nick. It's okay. Sometimes it feels good to let go. Let someone else in the driver's seat."

"I could say the same to you." His hands work their way down to my jockstrap again. I kind of wish he would breach the barrier. The unspoken line that's been drawn. But he never drifts past my waistband. "Maybe when this is over, you should take a turn in chastity."

"Maybe," Andre agrees with a light laugh. "But I'm not the one who always has my dick out."

"Maybe you should," I say without thinking.

He smiles down at me. "Would you like me to move lower?"

I close my eyes and nod. He stops rubbing my back. I hear him grab the bottle of oil, pop the cap and coat his hands with more liquid. I don't dare look at him. If I keep my eyes closed, this will all be like a dream, just a fantasy, with the sweet smells that surround me and the luxurious comfort of his bed.

Now warm hands are on my bottom. I hold my breath as I experience the strange new sensation. It's nice. Andre works my glutes, kneading his fingers into my muscles. I relax into the feeling, letting my mind drift.

Soon his fingers find their way to my darkest hidden places. I wanted him to wander there, but I would never ask. He gets to work massaging my hole. I'm tender and sensitive there. His touch is incredible.

"Is this okay?" he whispers into my ear.

"Yes," I breathe out.

Now all his attention is focused on this one small region. Yet the feeling radiates all through my body. He probes gently against my tightness, dipping his fingertips inside ever so carefully.

I sigh into the wonderful sensation. My cock twitches, pushes out another fat glob of sticky frustration. There's nowhere to go, and nowhere to grow. My foot-long is worthless, locked away in its little jail cell.

I let the frustration pour out of me, like warm waves on a beach, as they ebb and flow to other spaces in my body. All that energy seems to pool in the heat between my legs. I feel my hole relaxing as Andre works it into a warm, pliable doorway.

And just like that, his thick finger slips inside me. I shudder as he sweeps along my sweet spot. Oh, how I've missed that feeling. It's only been one day, but holding out hope that I'd get to feel it again is the only thing that's kept me from falling apart.

"I want more," I whisper.

"You do, huh?" Andre's voice pours over me like warm honey.

"Yes, please."

"How much more?"

"You know what I want..."

He tsks. "My how the power top has transformed into the greedy bottom. So soon, too." His voice is teasing me while his wicked finger taunts me from within. The way he tickles my swollen core sends me reeling. I grip the edge of his bed and bite down on my lip. "You're going to have to say the words."

"The words?"

"I won't do it without your consent."

I sigh. "I want you to fuck me, Andre. I want you to stick your dick all up inside me and I want you to fuck me until I cum. Please, Andre. I need it. I'm so frustrated and horny. I can't touch my dick, so I want yours. I want all of you."

Once the words start flowing, I can't stop myself. I sound just like the girls I pick up in the bars. The way I make them beg for my big cock. And now I'm the one desperate to be filled.

"Okay," Andre says soothingly. "First you're going to have to get me nice and wet."

My eyes snap open. I've never sucked another dude before. Never even thought about it. He slowly pulls his finger out of me. I let out a needy whine. He walks over to my face and unzips.

Out plops his cock, veiny and thick. It's not as big as mine, but plenty big enough, especially for a first-timer like me. I reach out and wrap my hand around his shaft. His cock is warm to the touch, the core soft and hard at once. I squeeze and stroke upward, rolling the skin over the crown.

He leans in closer. I swipe my tongue out, give it a tiny lick. I'm nervous, kind of afraid I won't like it. But when I taste the clean, fresh flavor on my palette, I'm instantly drawn in. I don't know what I expected, but Andre tastes wonderful. I can tell he takes good care of himself as I crane my head closer, smelling the soap in his groomed patch of wiry black curls.

His cock weighs heavy on my tongue. I let him slide inside, running my tongue all the way across the underside as I try to swallow him down. Then I close my lips around his girth and tease his head with a windshield-wiper effect. He shudders and lets out a moan that makes me beam with pride. I twirl my tongue around, then start bobbing up and down. My gag reflex kicks in when he goes too far, so I pull back and focus on planting kisses all over his flared cock head.

"You're very good at that," he says, petting my hair.

I hum my thanks and continue working down the length of him.

"Okay," he says, pulling away. "Are you ready for me to fill you up, Nick?"

My cock squeezes out a desperate teardrop. "Oh, god, yes."

Andre smiles widely and turns to the table beside his bed. He bends over, lending me a glimpse of his furry hole, and retrieves a condom from a drawer. I watch, mesmerized, as he tears open the wrapper and hands me the latex sheath. "Care to do the honors?"

"Gladly." I reach out, and his warm fingertips brush against mine during the exchange. He feels so good in my hands as I unroll the condom down the length of his cock.

He leans back and grabs a bottle of lube from the table, drizzles a generous amount over his big dick and works it into his fist. Then he steps behind me and gets on the bed. I can feel his heat as his body hovers over mine. He crouches down, rubs some lube into my hole. His finger dips inside, and I shiver at how nice it feels.

Then I feel the hardness of his cock knocking on my back door. I'm so nervous, yet I can't wait to let him inside. He presses firmly, sinks in slowly, and I feel myself spreading open for him. It burns a bit, hot and kind of sharp, but I breathe into the feeling and try to relax.

"You're doing great," he says.

I look over my shoulder. "Yeah?"

He leans closer and kisses me softly on my neck. I don't know what's come over me but I turn my head to meet his face and we just naturally seem to be drawn together, like two magnets. His warm mouth covers mine. I feel the softness of his lips with the contrast of his grainy beard stubble. His kiss is so dominating, and yet so nurturing. I whimper against him, and our tongues come out to play. All the while, he's sinking deeper inside me. His cock seems to summon electric pulses from my chute. His skin against mine, his entire length filling me to the brim.

"Oh, god," I sigh. I feel stuffed so full, it's nearly unbearable. But all that nervous tension breaks when the bulbous head of his cock pushes against my magic spot. "Ah, fuck, Andre."

"It's okay. Just breathe with me."

His chest heaves against my back. He thrusts deeper. The air is thick with the heady scent of his cologne. He's all around me and all inside me. I'm consumed by my frat bro. I never knew it could feel this good.

Andre starts bucking his hips, pounding all the way inside me and then pulling out. The rhythm fills me, and a fire is burning inside. First it's a small flame, then with each thrust, it's like he's lighting the kindling. The heat is rising, this stirring that I can't control. His weight holds me down, pinned to the bed beneath his hulking frame, his cock sliding in and out faster, harder, deeper.

The flames are burning out of control. Something stirs in my balls. The tension is too high. I break out into a sweat.

"Ah, Andre. Oh, fuuuck. Oh, my...fuck."

He reaches around and gently teases my nipples with his fingertips. Now the fire is burning inside me while a new sensation soars in my chest. My whole body is shaking with desire.

My nuts are aching, my big cock reduced to a weeping nub. I feel it crying a river of pre-cum between my legs. And I am helpless as Andre takes control of me. With each thrust, I feel myself closer to my breaking point. I'm completely undone, falling to pieces, yet I know I'm safe in his arms. I let myself let go, and then the fever breaks. A boiling geyser of cum explodes from my locked cock, splashing against my abs and creating a thick puddle beneath me.

"Oh, god, Andre," I mumble a string of nonsensical gibberish as my orgasm flows freely in waves.

"I'm cumming with you," Andre says, licking a path up my earlobe. "Ah, Nick." He breathes into my ear, and then I feel his cock stiffen and expand as he blows his load inside me. He keeps pumping, using my slick insides to squeeze out every last drop of his release.

When we're both drained of all the lust inside us, he collapses against my back. Our skin is sweaty and hot, pressed together. I feel us breathing in unison as our heart rates slow. His cock is still inside me, semi-hard but tucked in nice and snug. I close my eyes, feeling tired and satisfied. I could lie in his bed like this forever.

CHAPTER 8

28 Days Later

My time in chastity has come to an end. Some days were harder than others. Well, not *harder*. More like soft and frustrated. But Andre has made everything easier.

I never knew sex could feel this good, this deep and meaningful. All I ever knew was a life of quickies in some strange girl's bed. Because of my enormous size, I never had to put forth much effort. Just wham, bam, thank you, ma'am. Hell, they'd be lucky to get a 'thank you' from me. I was out the door before they could blink.

But it's totally different with Andre. A warmth blooms in my chest every time I think about him. We've been spending all our free time together. I miss him when we're apart, think about what he's doing when we're gone to our respective classes, and I wonder if he's thinking about me, too.

Is this all because I've been locked in chastity? It's strange to think a little cage made of metal could change me both inside and out. There are days I still crave the feeling of unloading my big cock inside a nice, warm hole. But the way Andre makes me feel is even better. It's not just a quickie, it's a slow burn that seems to go on and on as it consumes me.

Now it's time for the moment of truth. All the guys in my fraternity are gathered in the house, waiting for the big reveal. They insisted on witnessing my unlocking ceremony. I figured it was fair, considering they were forking over a thousand dollars of their own cash.

I stand in the middle of the circle, and they start up their chant. "Big Nick Energy! Big Nick Energy!"

Andre is there with me, a grin on his sexy face. His warm brown eyes gleam. "Take it all in, Nick. You've earned this."

"Thank you. I couldn't have done it without you." I smile and give a wink.

"You're certain Nick hasn't cheated?" Lucas asks.

"Yeah, he didn't steal the key and sneak out to pound some babe?" Jon adds.

Andre turns and addresses the skeptics in the room. "I can honestly say with absolute certainty that Nick never had access to the key. I kept it hidden in a secure location the entire time. And there's no way he got out of his cage. Let's say, just for example, he did manage to slip out some way. Even though he'd be free, the lock would still be snapped together. He wouldn't be able to get it back on. So I know for certain Nick has won this bet, fair and square. He never unlocked, and he hasn't hooked up with any girls this month."

I have to suppress a laugh. It's not like Andre is lying.

"So now, I will do the honors." Andre takes my caged manhood in his warm hand and slides the key into the lock. It's sweet relief as he unhinges the metal and pulls the tube piece off my shaft.

My cock balloons up in an instant. It's an amazing feeling. I'm not even embarrassed that all my bros are watching as my cock grows in front of their eyes. In fact, I feel damn proud. I place my hands behind my head and swing my foot-long cock back and forth for all to see. My meat makes a satisfying slap against my thighs as I whip it from side to side. Every inch of me is still there, all twelve of them.

"Big Nick Energy! Big Nick Energy! Big Nick Energy!!!" My frat bros go wild, clapping and hooting as I put on a show. Then I spin my dick around like an airplane propeller, and they erupt into laughter.

This feels good. Really good. I love being part of this crazy, melting pot of a frat house. I love the connection, the trust, the strange sort of intimacy I never knew I could have with a group of guys. And there's one man in particular who deserves all my gratitude.

"Why don't you guys set out the drinks and order some pizzas," I say. "I'm footing the bill tonight." This earns another round of cheers. "I need to go upstairs for a few minutes and then we'll get this party going."

I nod for Andre to follow me. When I step into his bedroom, the air is thick with the smell of his vanilla candles and his woodsy, fresh cologne. I love this space. I'm thinking about asking if I can swap places with his roommate. That would give us a lot more privacy.

Nobody knows what we've been doing. We've been sneaking around in secret, keeping things on the down-low.

"How do you feel?" Andre asks, taking my hands into his.

"Incredible, but..." There's hesitation written all over my face, and I know Andre can see it. He nods, his warm chocolate-brown eyes encouraging me to share. I feel like I can tell him anything. "I thought it would be great to be set free. I've been counting the days, honestly. But now that I am, well... I feel naked now. I miss the weight of the cage as it holds me down. I miss the security of being locked. I'm wondering what you would say if I asked you to lock me back up. And keep the key."

A smile fills Andre's face. "You want me to be your key holder?"

"If that's what you call it."

"Nick, that would be..." He shakes his head. "So incredible. I was hoping you'd feel this way, but I didn't want to pressure you. It had to be something you came up with on your own."

I feel like my heart is dancing in my chest. "Really? You don't think it's weird?"

"Not at all." He plants a big kiss on my mouth, and we hold each other tight. A few minutes pass, and we just stay this way. I enjoy the heat of our bodies pressed together. But my stubborn cock responds with a raging hard-on. Andre looks at the obscene protrusion and chuckles. "Down boy."

"What about us?" I ask suddenly. I couldn't hold the words inside anymore. "Can we keep seeing each other?"

"So this isn't just about being your key holder?"

"Not for me, it isn't."

"I'm just... Wow. I'm kind of speechless." Andre smiles and shakes his head again. "Nick, the player. Big Nick Energy. I never would have pegged you for the type who wants to be locked in chastity."

"You've helped me find something deeper. More fulfilling."

He kisses me again. Long and slow. I can sense everything he's feeling just by the way his lips melt into mine. When we finally pull apart for air, he says, "I'll keep you locked up as long as you like. If it's ever too much, you just say the words. I'll set you free."

"Don't ever set me free, Andre." I pull him tight against me.

"Don't worry, Nick. I'm not going anywhere."

And with this, my heart is locked down for Andre. My cock isn't the only part of me he's taken captive. We kiss again, sealing our fate.

"Wanna go downstairs and tell the guys?" he asks.

"About us? Yes," I say, my heart soaring. "But the cage will be our special secret. It's just for you and me."

I get undressed and offer Andre my twelve inches to lock up. He asks if I want to take it for a spin first, a little joyride. But I shake my head. The only kind of pleasure I want to feel is what comes from inside me. The only dick I want to satisfy is his.

It's not easy coaxing myself into the cage, but with some determination we finally get my trouser monster tucked in tight. The click of the lock is music to my ears. I pull my pants back up. Andre takes my hand in his, and we make our way downstairs to announce our relationship to the guys. Now every part of me belongs to him.

ALSO AVAILABLE FROM NATHAN BAY

King of the Sea

The Invisible Plan

Young Forever

Bathhouse Confessions

Bathhouse Confessions 2

Bathhouse Confessions 3

Bathhouse Confessions XXL

Freshman Fantasies

Prostate Pounder XXL

Visit <u>amazon.com/author/nathanbay</u> for news + info.